Racing Apollo

Daniel C. Owen

Cover art and design by Susan Owen Kagan
skagan@shaw.ca
Copy editing by Bailey Harman
Formatting by Polgarus Studio

The author can be contacted at racingapollo1@gmail.com

To my wife, Jacqueline, for her love and support.

PROLOGUE

'The Oracle gave an oracle at the Oracle'

501 B.C.E

"Death."

His judgement. Binding and unrelenting. Averting his eyes, the general cradled his new-born son, stroking the thick, red hair.

Sparta was a society only for soldiers, every male and female lived and trained for battle. Nothing less was acceptable.

Preparations had already been made.

He stood at the bottom of the mountain. Lifting his baby to the sky, he cursed the gods and fixed his gaze on the setting sun.

"Apollo," he said, "your oracle was a lie. The oracle told of my son as a leader, a saviour of Greece. Not this. How could you have let this happen to me?"

He placed the baby in the tripod, careful to avoid

brushing the damaged limb against the ragged edges of the beaten bronze pot. From the pocket of his tunic he withdrew a tiny egg-shaped stone. Laying it in his son's palm he hung his head, as the tiny fingers curled around it.

He was about to lift the tripod when a youthful hand tugged on his tunic.

"Allow me the honour, father."

He nodded and turned away, as his infant son was dragged up the side of the mountain, left for the wolves.

CHAPTER ONE

493 B.C.E

The water droplets fell onto the goat's exposed skin and it trembled, then struggled with the rawhide ties binding its legs. Nodding to his aide, the Spartan general drew his hand across the shaved strip of skin traversing the goat's belly, calming it. His aide withdrew a bronze dagger and the general grasped it handle first, careful to avoid contact with the sharpened blade.

The goat's belly split open smoothly, and when its eyes clouded over, the general closed the lids. Spreading the flesh apart, the general grunted as he examined the entrails. All were in prime condition. He cut a piece off the liver and placed it in a fold in his tunic. It would please his patrons.

Scooping the entrails into his hands, he lifted them high over his head, and approached the priestess' chamber. He stopped at the foot of the stairs and stood in a warrior's stance, feet shoulder length apart, balanced and leaning slightly to the side. Although not especially muscular, his lean frame was solid. The goat's blood dripping into his eyes matched his hair, which curled down around his shoulders, the top tied by a strip of snakeskin into a side-lock. Wiping the blood from his brow, he began the blessing.

"Blessed be Apollo, Creator of Light. I give to you this sacrifice, may its aroma sweeten your palate, and may you in turn bestow honour and glory upon our city."

Bowing low, he climbed the short staircase leading to the priestess sitting on her tripod, placed the entrails at her feet and backed down again to stand stiffly beside his aide.

Clothed in white cotton, the priestess brushed a grey hair from her forehead with a gnarled hand. She placed her hand back on the omphalos, a brittle egg shaped stone bound loosely with white threads, which she wound around her fingers. In her other hand she held a small branch cut from a laurel tree.

She poked at the offering with the branch, her dress brushing the carcass, bloodying the hem, and answered the general's blessing with her own.

"Blessed be Apollo, Creator of Light. I am his Oracle. I give his oracle. Blessed be the Oracle."

Breaking the skin of the heart she inserted her index finger and removed it from the pile, placing it at the base of the omphalos. With her bloodied finger she unwound a string, and yanked it taught.

"This string, general, is your fate and the fate of your city. It is strong, unyielding, unbending, like your city. But if it is cut, it severs and is destroyed. Always remember, Apollo is your master, and he can destroy you."

The general's aide drew his sword, but the general placed a hand on his shoulder. Jumping back and wincing in remembered pain, the aide sheathed his weapon.

"Do not threaten me priestess. You are trying my patience. I am not a peasant asking about my crop. I am not a fool colonist trying to find new lands. I paid handsomely for this private oracle, given a prime sacrifice, and recited the proper blessing. Let me ask my question, give me my answer, and we will be on our way."

The priestess unwound another length of string, lifted it high above her head, and glared at the Spartans. Her clear blue eyes shone with a hint of yellow.

"You need not ask your question general. Apollo has already provided me with the answer. Accept my oracle. Suspend your disbelief."

Sitting back on her tripod, she intertwined her legs among the metallic supports and rewound the thread. Tearing at her hair and moaning, her eyes rolled back in her head, and she felt the power surge.

It had been sixty odd years since her mother brought her to the temple, claiming refuge. She had volunteered her services to Apollo in exchange for a home. Not having a city to claim as your own was a searing shame, she had been ostracised, rejected by all.

Her mother never spoke of her life before the temple and always kept her head bowed in front of the priests and priestess, but she taught her daughter to watch, observe and absorb countless offerings, prayers, and requests. And to recognise and befriend the dozens of informants and spies bred through a thousand years of temple attendants and their families.

By the time she was fifteen her daughter could rely on any temple source to answer all the questions put to the current priestess, and two years later when the priestess died unexpectedly, her daughter was a logical replacement.

She focused her attention back on her audience and in high, cackling tones began to babble, then formed her words and hurled them at the Spartans like lightning bolts.

"I am Apollo, believe in me General. I know your question and your secret. Your spies have informed you that the Persians are preparing for invasion. You do not know when or where. They will invade in three years. The coastline is long, impossible to guard. They are powerful. You will need help. Look to Athens. Athenians and Spartans together can defeat them."

"Never!" The Spartan general drew his sword and smashed the flat side against one of the marble columns. "Athenians are weaklings. They cannot match us in power and strength. Ally with them? It is unthinkable."

Unwinding the thread again, the priestess stretched it in front of her and moaned, vapours from the fissures under the tripod swirling around her.

"You are wrong. Your ego has grown too large. Do not defy me. I am still your god. You think you are my equal. You do not believe. You even choose to rename yourself Hades. The Lord of the Underworld will not be pleased.

Turning to his aide, the general again gripped his shoulder, squeezing powerfully this time, and the aide sank to his knees.

"You Pantheras, were the only one who knew," he hissed. "Who did you tell?"

Pantheras wrenched his shoulder free and with his good arm ripped his tunic open, exposing his chest.

"No one I swear, general. My loyalty is to you alone. If you question it, take the knife, slit me open, and examine my heart. I am a true son of Sparta. I will not quiver."

Releasing his aide the general pulled at his side-lock. "That is not necessary Pantheras. I spoke in haste. Spartan loyalty is beyond question."

He fingered his sword and glared at the priestess.

"You are correct priestess, or Apollo, or whoever you claim to be right now. I do not believe. However my patrons still believe in the gods. They insisted I seek your counsel and guidance. I had no choice. They finance my army."

"And your army still believes," the priestess said.

She relaxed her grip on the thread and leaned forward. Tossing her head, she shook the fine-spun cotton off her face. Her heavily wrinkled skin was almost translucent, as if the slightest touch would cause it to rip and tear.

"Yes," replied the general. "The fools. Afraid not of death, but their soul barred entrance to the Underworld. Forced to wander the depths of the earth for eternity by Lord Hades."

Leaping up the short staircase the general ripped the thread out of the priestess' hands and wound it around the handle of a short knife he produced from the inside of his tunic. Lashing out, he nicked the priestess' neck, and grinned as she closed her hands around her own throat.

"This charade can stop right now, priestess. Your blood flows like mine. You lack any special powers except for your sources. If my patrons had not sent me, I would have approached you on my own."

"No one has ever dared assault me," said the priestess. "It is an attack on Apollo himself."

The general reached out and wrenched one of the priestess' hands free from her throat. Twisting her wrist, he bent it back, extending the pressure up her arm to the socket.

"Think of this arm as your fate, priestess of Apollo. Power and strength, not belief, holds your destiny. Others may believe the gods walk with them, but I learned long ago to go my own way. No god will aid you, rid you of your pain. Only me."

The priestess struggled to rise from her tripod, but sank down as the general lifted her arm up, pointing it to the ceiling. The blood from her throat had stemmed, and she tore at her hair with one hand in frustration.

"My attendants, my chief priests. They will bear witness to this attack. Your punishment shall be swift."

"Call them priestess," the general said, winking at his aide. "Better yet, Pantheras. You raise the alarm."

Pantheras unsheathed his sword and smashed the flat side of the blade against the edge of the tripod. The shrill shriek of bronze on bronze reverberated through the cold marble columns with no answer.

"You see priestess, we come prepared as always. I offered your priests one choice only. Loyalty to me. They chose well. Now they wear red robes instead of white. Your polished theatrics have worked well for you and your kind, but they cannot match a sharpened blade. There is no one left except you. And your web of informants and spies. A valuable network indeed, and one I intend to take advantage of with a priestess of my own. My daughter."

Stifling a cry, the priestess ripped her arm from the general's grasp and tore another thread loose from the omphalos.

"This is your life, this is your life," she intoned. "Do not aspire to immortality. It is not for mortals. Once this thread is severed your life is forfeit to Apollo."

The general ran the knife along the edge of the thread. Whispers of white cotton floated to the floor.

"You are wrong, priestess. My army will know me as Hades. My daughter will be priestess to Apollo. And my son will be…"

His voice shook, the blade falling away from the thread. Looking down at the omphalos he regained his composure, his voice rising in challenge until it raged off the temple roof and floor.

"My son, my strong, healthy son will be known as Cerberus, guardian of my realm, guardian of the underworld. All shall fear him."

He ran his finger across the dried blood on the priestess' neck. Meeting his gaze, the priestess slumped on her tripod, the yellow in her pupils intensifying.

"You must face your fate general as I must face mine. Do not dismiss my oracle. You must ally with Athens. You must combine your armies to defeat the Persians. Otherwise all of Greece will be lost."

The general grunted and nodded. "Perhaps that is wise advice for commanders of other cities, other armies, but not a Spartan. However, a good commander builds upon even the most distasteful information and uses it to advantage."

Raising his hand over the priestess' head, she shrank, lifting her good arm as a shield.

"No, do not cower, priestess. You have lived a long life and that is to be commended," the general said, pushing her arm aside, gently entwining his fingers in her wispy hair.

"Your oracle has merit. Athens will look to us for help when the invasion comes."

"Yes, like I, I mean Apollo said. Three years from now."

Her eyelids closed as the general stroked her temples.

"Rest for a moment priestess. You deserve this momentary peace. Listen well. Relay my plan to Apollo. We are now at peace with Athens, but our help will not be forthcoming. We will allow the Persians to invade. Athens will beseech us for help and it will be offered, but when they march out to fight we will somehow be delayed, and the Persians will destroy Athens's army."

Opening her eyes, the priestess jerked herself upright, but the general forced her back onto her stool beside the tripod.

"Then we will smash a weakened Persian army and continue on to Athens. Without their army, Athens will be ours finally, as it should have been these past thousand years."

"No," the priestess said. "Apollo speaks through me. It is not his wish, not his plan. Do not defy him. He is your god."

The general grabbed his aide's sword and smashed it on

the side of the tripod, denting both, then tossed it aside. Brushing back his side-lock from his forehead, he knelt, withdrew his knife and levelled it at the priestess' chest.

"Apollo does not exist priestess. If he did he would prevent me from doing this," he said, plunging the knife into the priestess' heart, withdrawing it only when her lifeless body spread flat beside the tripod.

Closing her eyes, he pressed his mouth close to her ear. "And he would have prevented me from assuming his brother's name. Call me Hades, priestess, when your soul comes to drink at the river of souls. That is, if Cerberus is generous and lets you in."

Rising, he unwound the thread from the priestess' fingers and placed it loosely on the omphalos. Tapping the egg-shaped stone lightly with the edge of his sword, he lifted his blade, and swung it down viciously. Shards scattered around their feet and threads floated to the ground.

"You see, priestess. No thunderbolt from the heavens."

His voice rose, bouncing off the marble walls. "Only me. I shall be known as Hades. Defier of gods. Ruler of Sparta. And I shall smash Athens and the Persians like I destroyed you and the trappings of Apollo."

Leaping up the steps, Pantheras extended his hand. "Let me be the first to address you formally as Hades. Your vision, your planning, all have come to pass. Nothing can stop us now."

Hades put a finger to the lips of his aide and gestured towards a shadow rising off a ledge hidden high on a back wall. The shadow tip-toed down almost invisible stairs and edged towards a corner. Stroking his side-lock, Hades pointed his sword at it.

Pantheras lifted one foot quietly but brought it down on one of the stone chips from the shattered omphalos and its crack caused the shadow to start running, sprinting towards the far end of the chamber. It emerged into the torchlight, exposing a thatch of blond hair and long, slender legs before disappearing through an arched doorway.

Hades restrained his aide. "He is too fast for you."

An admiring grin spread across his face. "With that speed he should be in the Games."

"What of our plan?" Pantheras said. "Your priests are going to be telling people a Persian force killed the priestess."

Hades stroked his side-lock. "The youth will be eliminated. It will be a good test for my son. There are not many around with hair that colour, and that temple rat no longer has a home. People will dismiss him."

Grasping the handle with both hands, Hades raised the knife above his head then smashed the flat edge against the tripod's rim, bending the blade. Palming the handle he fingered the dolphin symbols, favoured by Persian warriors, spun it and dropped it at the priestess' feet.

"Come, Pantheras. Back to camp. I'm afraid we are in for some alarming news."

Pausing at the entrance, Hades pounded his fist into his palm and spit onto the cold marble.

"Apollo, you do not walk beside me. You do not exist. Once Athens falls, all of Greece will follow me and realise the power and mortality of the sword. They will forget the gods. My revenge shall be complete."

CHAPTER TWO

Dip sprinted through the temple, his long legs moving in a rhythm that could not be taught, only admired. His calf muscles protested slightly at the speed, the lack of a warm up, and Dip grimaced but did not slow.

Who can help me now? he thought. It's always been the priestess.

She had accepted him as a child. Desperately ill, all he could remember was the pounding in his chest and his mother's soothing tones. "Look to Apollo," she said. "Bathe in his waters as I have. They will heal your heart. Forgive me my son, I had no choice, no choice."

His mother could not stay. The trip back to her city was long and arduous and she did not survive. At least that was what the priestess told him. Now he was in his fourteenth year, and his daily baths in the spring had relieved him of his pain.

But as he reached the columns lining the temple entrance he thought he felt a twinge in his chest and paused, massaging his heart. There was no pursuit, no scrape of foot armour echoing along the marble floors. No voices rising in challenge.

Dip had seen almost every part of Greece come to the temple seeking their oracle. Of course the priestess had answers for all. A Corinthian merchant advised to sell his grapes to the barbarians. Colonists told to establish towns along Greece's northern borders. Even a haughty gold seeker given elaborate directions to a mountain within Persia. Reactions to the oracles were mixed, ranging from meek acceptance to amusement. Some politicians offered bribes for a favourable answer. Accepted as "special offerings" to Apollo, the politicians (dependent upon the size of the "offering") left satisfied.

All of these Dip had witnessed from the ledge, hidden behind the priestess' platform. Part of your education, she constantly reminded him, aside from studying the Gods and heroes like Heracles.

He often imagined himself like Heracles, chasing down the Erymanthian Boar; wrestling the Giant, Antaeus; or his greatest test; defeating and dragging Cerberus from Hades, into the light. And Zeus' final reward, immortality.

The temple columns glistened in the bright sunlight and in the distance through the valley the deep blue of the Aegean melted into the hills. Dip loved being high on the mountain and he often prayed he could stay forever. Now the Spartans would surely come after him.

Glancing up to the sun he shook out his arms and legs. Far overhead he saw a raven burst out of a cloudbank, rise, and disappear into the sun. The sun's warmth folded around him and the ache in his heart disappeared. He started to run. Not a panic induced sprint, but a controlled, measured jog designed to work, strengthen and train, not strain his heart. It was a pace Dip improved on every day and it was his joy, his escape from the confines of Apollo's temple.

Force of habit carried him along his familiar route down the road past the stadium cut into the side of the mountain. As he ran, he saw a few competitors outside stretching, waiting to practice their sprints, and they did not notice him. Others had finished and were scraping the dirt and sweat off their bodies with strigils. Dip tried a discarded blade once but threw it aside; too many cuts. He preferred bathing in his stream.

In a few hours the stadium would be full, banners from a dozen cities stretching from section to section, their emblems and colours proudly displayed. Every four years Delphi hosted the Pythian Games and all of Greece united towards a common goal, victory at the Games, second only to the honours earned in the Olympics. Various athletic events were contested but the glory an athlete received, the honour most coveted, came in the sprints. Dip had learned the names of former champions and had carved them in a discarded limestone slab outside the stadium.

Dip longed to run in the Games and he stopped at the slab, tracing his fingers over space reserved for the next champion, saying as usual, a quick prayer to Nike, goddess of victory.

"You, boy."

Dip jerked his hand from the wall and turned. A lithe,

muscular, young woman lay on her back, one leg flat, the other stretched into the air. She was spilling drops from a small clay pot onto the back of her thigh; the pungent aroma cut through the air, snapping Dip's head back.

"Come here boy, hold my leg up. My hamstring pulls at me. I have a race to win."

Dip paused and glanced back up the road to the temple.

"Now!" she said. "I am Kheerna of Sparta, thrice city champion. Assist me, or suffer my wrath!"

Dip backed up and began to run. The cursing and footsteps came quickly behind him and he began to sprint, then heard a lightning bolt-like 'crack' and an exclamation of pain as the cursing faded away.

Glancing around, Dip smiled. His run had carried him away from the stadium and back up the mountain on a side road distant from the temple, but one he had used innumerable times.

He jogged to some laurel trees stretched down the side of the road. Their skinny branches threw sparse shadows and Dip plunged between two of the largest trees onto a trail no wider than his shoulders. Lining it were more trees, each bowed at the top-their branches interlocked.

Cool air drifted down to him and he slowly walked towards the opening cut into the mountainside only a few paces away. He paused at the entrance, inhaling the musty fumes from the stream. It flowed from a small opening in one wall of the cave into a tunnel on the far side. Dip stripped off his tunic and stepped into the water, immersing his legs and torso up to his chin. Tiny swirling eddies bounced against his limbs, and wriggling himself between two small stones into a slight form fitting depression worn into the polished stream bed, he sighed, the same way he had sighed when he had first discovered Apollo's stream.

At least that was what he had called it. It was more than his secret. He had no city. Apollo's temple was dominated by the priestess and no matter how kind she was, it was not his home. Tracing his fingers across the polished lip of the bank, a small piece broke away cutting his finger. He pressed his finger to his cheek and cried. This stream had been his comfort, his home. Now his world was crumbling. There was no safe refuge. Dragging himself out of the steamy water he lay down and let the weariness overcome him.

His first morning after his mother left him at the temple a raven had called to him from a nest hidden in the temple roof and he swivelled quickly, catching a glimpse of its black wings as it swept up the mountain. Rushing down the temple steps he had sprinted after it, but pains racked his chest and he stopped.

The next day it reappeared through the mist, circling a few paces beyond his reach. He raced after it again and once more the pains started and he had to stop while the bird perched on the top of a nearby olive tree. After a few minutes he again tried, this time at a walk. No pains, but he could not catch the raven who stayed just ahead of him. After an hour of walking he returned to the temple.

"That was Apollo's bird," the priestess had explained as she wiped the tears from his face. "No one except Heracles can catch one. You don't believe me. Come. I will tell you a story from The Labours. Listen and learn. Pray to Apollo."

The pattern continued. Each day the raven was circling, waiting for him, and he walked after it a little faster than before. This continued for a number of weeks until he was finally able to run slowly, sustaining his pace. He progressed rapidly and still the raven flew on, leading him on longer and longer runs.

Every day he raced the raven, who remained just out of reach, imagining himself as Heracles, slaying and capturing ferocious beasts.

One year later, as he ran after it, concentrating only on his pace, judging his own strength and endurance, the raven led him around the mountain for an hour and then headed back to the temple. It stopped at a row of laurel trees, its leaves reflecting the sun's rays into his face. Flying through an opening between two of the largest trees it led him to the cave and the stream. Immersing himself in the stream's churning eddies, he felt the last traces of his chest pains disappear. The raven flew down the tunnel opening at the far end of the cave and he had not seen it since, nor felt any ache in his chest. Until today.

As Dip drifted off, the vapours hovering over one of the eddies swirled, moving slowly across the water. Dip rubbed his eyes but the sulphurous water stung, causing them to tear. Hundreds of yellow pin-sized suns spun within the vortex, which slowed and collapsed into itself, merging sun with sun, until all that remained were two tiny yellow orbs floating on the surface. Dip peered over the edge of the bank and sucked in his breath.

The priestess' face stared back at him. Not the hard, haggard and lined visage he was used to, but one that was fresh and lucid. Dip grabbed his tunic and cleared his eyes of tears, and the vision changed, became indistinct and blurred.

"Wait," Dip said. "Priestess, I am lost without you. Tell me what to do."

"Look at me," said the priestess and her blue eyes came back into focus, blazing with twin suns. Her words were clear and precise, but her lips did not move.

"I have made my share of mistakes and even though I will soon find myself dwelling in the underworld, Apollo and I are at peace. You cannot find shelter with me any longer. Apollo has given me your oracle. Listen well. Be ready. Be prepared."

Dip thrust his hands into the water and they passed through the reflection without disturbing the features. The water was icy cold and he withdrew them, shivering.

"Tell me priestess," he said. "I am cold. I want only to go home."

The priestess' eyes blurred slightly, then cleared. Her voice rang clearly in Dip's ears.

"Dip, your path is filled with danger. You must warn Athens of the Spartan's plan. Athens must be prepared for Persia's invasion. Run for Athens, race for victory. Race Apollo for your destiny."

Dip wrapped his arms around his shoulders trying to still his shaking body and chattering teeth.

"Priestess, I don't know any Athenians. How can I warn

them? I can't run for them either. I do not belong to their city. I do not belong to any city. How am I supposed to do this? How do I race Apollo?"

The priestess' eyes broke from Dip and fixed on the tunnel entrance. Dip saw the stylised runner, arms thrust into the air etched into the stones over the opening.

"Nike. Victory."

"Yes," said the priestess. "This is your oracle. When your spirit must rise in victory shout her name. Look to Cassandra for help and Odysseus to lead. Be like Heracles, Dip. Challenge Cerberus. Race Apollo for your victory. Race Apollo for your destiny."

"But Odysseus is just a little boy, and his arm …"

Dip stopped and stared back into the stream. The priestess' image was swirling, sucking back into the murky water until the last of the yellow orbs disappeared. Dip shut his eyes tight, forcing flashes of searing light beneath his eyelids trying to recapture her presence, but the pressure was too intense and exhausted, he lay down beside the stream and slept.

He awoke shivering, and quickly pulled on a fresh white tunic he kept as a change of clothing after a long run. The stream had calmed and again was hot to the touch. Glancing up at the tunnel entrance he saw the runner and approached it, lifting his fingers close, stopping when he heard the sounds coming from the tunnel.

High pitched yips echoed, followed by a long mournful penetrating howl. Dip backed away as it intensified, hurling up from the depths of the tunnel like a gush of wind and he put his hand to his heart.

Dip tumbled backwards out of the cave, coming to rest in a blown pile of laurel leaves. Scrambling to his feet, he sprinted down the path and dove through the border of trees onto the middle of the road.

Clouds covered the midday sun and a dark mist seemed to roll up from around the bend. Dip squinted and sniffed the air. A faint oily scent reached him and he began to run back down the road. Glancing behind, he noticed the mist closing on him, and his teeth ground on particles of dirt and grit.

Not mist he realised, but dirt churning into the air and he froze, staring at a group of Spartan warriors in full battle gear charging towards him.

CHAPTER THREE

Dip stared at the Spartans bearing down on him. There were three of them, each wearing a bronze helmet feathered with a white plume. Metal from the helmet extended over their cheekbones and a thin strip detailed with gold filigree covered their noses. Each warrior carried a large bronze shield decorated with snakes. Shinguards also made of bronze reached to the tops of their kneecaps and their green tunics extended to their upper thighs.

Dip could see the muscles on their thighs tighten as they ran. But something was missing.

"Don't just stand there, move!" a voice said.

The Spartans were about twenty strides away, running as fast as Dip had seen anyone run, even with all the heavy armour they were wearing.

"Oh Apollo, why did you make this one so timid?"

A hand grabbed his arm and he landed on the side of the road as the Spartans thundered past without even a sidelong glance.

"Faster you slackers, faster," yelled the lead runner, who

put on a burst of speed. As they faded from view Dip could still clearly hear his angry bellow, "Do you want to be champions or not?"

Dip turned to the person who pulled him to safety. It was a girl slightly older than himself and taller. Her skin was golden brown and her dark curls fell below her shoulders. Perhaps her most distinctive feature were her brown, almond shaped eyes, locked on the now distant Spartans in an intensity that forced him to lower his head.

"Cassandra, I should have known it was you."

Straightening into a warrior's stance, Cassandra pulled Dip to his feet. Her only weapon was a dagger which she quickly produced from a leather thong fitted underneath her tunic.

"What were you doing, standing in the middle of the road like that? They would have run you over without remembering enough for a good laugh over a few draught back at their camp."

Dip hung his head. "I was scared. I thought they were coming after me."

"After you? Why would you think that?"

"I'll explain it to you while we go back into town. We need to find Odysseus. I promise to keep my wits about me if we run into those Spartans again."

"Don't worry about that," Cassandra said. "I've been trailing them since this morning. Didn't you notice anything unusual about what they were wearing, or did your eyes lose their courage too?"

Dip swallowed and stared at the ground, hoping a hole

would miraculously appear and swallow him up.

"Uh, let's see. They had their helmets, tunics, shields, sandals, swords. That's it. None of them were wearing swords. A Spartan always has a sword with him."

"Except when they're in training for a race," Cassandra added. "And that's what those three have been doing since this morning. The swords are too cumbersome to train with. They would be tripping every third step."

"Of course, they must be preparing for the sprints. Polymestor from Miletos, Philon from Korkyra, Meneptolemos from Apollonia. All champions."

Dip's voice quickened with each name. "Meneptolemos, now there was a runner. I'd give anything to compete. Anything. Think of the honours, the glory. I'd fly past my competition."

"Even if you could fly, you would never dare beat a Spartan. Why you're nothing but a temple rat."

Dip sank back down to the road. Grabbing a handful of dirt he rubbed it into his scalp and shaking, smeared it under his eyes.

"Dip, what's wrong?"

Dip tried to rip his tunic at the shoulder but Cassandra grabbed his hand and lowered it to his waist.

"Spartans murdered the priestess," he said.

Cassandra silently cursed herself. Sitting down, she put one arm around his waist and rocking him softly, started brushing the soil out of his hair. She hummed a blessing to Apollo and watched the dust rise from his hair. Keeping her voice low, her sombre tones rose slightly with each refrain in cadence with the brushing of her hand, until she was satisfied all the dirt was gone, settled back to the ground.

"Still your heart, Dip," she said. "It beats too fast, you must calm down."

I should have known.

It's been three years since I smeared earth in my hair and on my face. Three years since I covered the windows and mirrors. My dreams still smell of rotted vegetables and Spartan blood.

My people, my family. Helots the Spartans called us. Less than slaves. Dirt beneath their feet. Fit only for grubbing out a few sparse fields of vegetables in the desert for the almighty Spartan soldiers.

It should have been easy. We outnumbered our oppressors sevenfold. My parents knew this. Meetings were held. Plans made. Weapons stolen and stored. But we were found out.

Cassandra paused. Dip's eyes met hers and he lay his head on her lap.

"Please Cassandra," he said. "Remove the last of the dirt for me."

Gently she searched through the straw coloured hair, removing the smallest particles of soil.

No one knew how we were discovered and it did not matter. The Spartans came without warning. My parents tried to hide me and my brother Castor in the garbage cart, but they were too slow. Dragged through the street we were forced onto the ground. My parents were brave; they did not utter a sound, even as the spears passed through their throats. We were spared.

Castor was only in his sixth year but he was large for his age. They ripped him from my arms, threw him into a group of older boys and carted them away. "We'll come back for you in a couple of years," they taunted. I mourned my parents as was customary, and tried to find my brother, but I was too weak and the other survivors too fearful. My path took me here to Delphi and when I am ready I will reclaim my brother and exact my revenge.

Ruffling Dip's hair, Cassandra lifted him to his feet.

"I'm glad you came to Delphi, Cassandra," Dip said. "You could beat any Spartan. And I would be there by your side."

The hard edges in Cassandra's face vanished and she laughed. "I can look after myself. Anyways, some help you're going to be, standing like a statue whenever a Spartan's around. You would be as much help as Odysseus and you realise of course that is no compliment."

"Odysseus," Dip said. "Cassandra, I have to tell you why I thought those Spartans were after me and we must find Odysseus."

Cassandra placed her hands on Dip's shoulders and locked his eyes with hers. "Dip, I understand about the priestess and I'm sorry, but I have more important things to do than try to find one strange, little boy. An important Spartan delegation is in town for the Games. I am going to concentrate on them. Don't get in my way."

"Listen to me," Dip said. "You are part of this as well. It is something that we all must do."

"By whose command? I don't take orders from you or

anyone else. I answer only to myself. Now, I'm going to find those Spartans."

As she passed Dip she leaned her shoulder into his chest, knocking him down.

"Cassandra, this isn't my idea. It is my oracle."

"Your oracle." Cassandra stopped and lifted Dip to his feet. "Tell me more."

She listened attentively as Dip retold the events from the Temple. Finishing with the priestess' message at the stream, he turned to face Cassandra. Although she was only a few months older, he was anxious for her opinion and longed for her approval.

"I will help you, Dip," she said. "I don't care what happens to the Athenians and I don't know what it means or even how you can race Apollo or challenge Cerberus, but I'm afraid of what would happen to the rest of Greece if the Spartans succeed. No one should suffer like my people. This will be a great opportunity for me to hit at the Spartans hard. You can count on me to the death."

Dip knew she was not being overly dramatic.

"Well?"

"My future depends on this too," Dip said.

They walked along the road without speaking until they could see the stadium below them. People were filing into it, finding places to sit still bathed in the sun, away from the shadows, eager for the evening's competition to begin. Dip was not sure what was being contested but he recognised a group of people walking towards the entrance. Most wore brightly coloured tunics. Except for one. His tunic was a plain grey and he carried a shield bearing a likeness of Athena, patron goddess of Athens.

"There are the Athenians. All I have to do is reach them and tell them about the oracle. Come on Cassandra."

"No Dip, wait. Don't you see?"

Dip was already far ahead of her. Reaching the stadium's entrance he searched desperately for the Athenians. The crowd thinned and he heard a roar that seemed to shake the ground beneath him. It was no use, the competitors were being introduced which meant the Athenians were already inside. There was no way in for him, only citizens of Delphi or guests from other cities were allowed as spectators. A hand clamped onto his shoulder and he hung his head.

"I'm sorry Cassandra," he began. "I should have waited for you, but this was my big chance to warn the Athenians about Sparta. Now what do I do?"

Dip was spun around and he fell, face down. A foot pinned him to the ground. Rubbing the dirt from his eyes he said, "Cassandra, I've already apologised, what more do you want?"

Pain shot through his side as the flat edge of a sword struck him.

"To start with, my name isn't Cassandra."

Dip's vision cleared. Standing over top of him was a large youth, with piercing black eyes and long red hair, holding a shield and a short sword. Around him were two other boys similarly armed. Serpents decorated their shields.

"My name is Cerberus, and these two are Jackal and Wolf, my hounds."

CHAPTER FOUR

Dip was jerked to his feet by the smallest boy, Wolf, who pressed the tip of his sword against Dip's throat. The skin broke easily and a drop of blood slid down onto his chest.

"Give me the order, sir," he said. "I will finish him for General Hades myself."

"No," Cerberus commanded. "My father wants him alive, at least until he has had a chance to question him."

"About what?" Jackal said. He was almost as tall as Cerberus but not as muscled. "What could he know that would be of any value? Even now his knees are shaking like those of a helot."

Jackal began to laugh and Wolf pushed Dip back to the ground, his sword poised for a final thrust.

"Watch how easily my blade penetrates, Cerberus. Your father would be proud."

"Silence," Cerberus said. "Have you forgotten your training? We do not question any order put to us by a superior."

Stepping to Wolf's side, he grabbed the smirking boy's

sword arm at the wrist and twisted it back until a loud pop was heard at the shoulder, the sword falling to the ground. Holding on to the arm, now hanging limp, he drew Wolf's face close to his own.

"Now, tell me proper Spartan procedure for reaction to pain."

Wolf stiffened and wrenched his arm free. "A Spartan does not react, sir."

"Good," said Cerberus. "Do not worry about your shoulder, it can easily be put back into place. Then the pain will stop. Would you like me to do it now?"

"Thank you sir. I can wait until we get back to camp."

Cerberus nodded. "That was the correct answer."

Dip was horrified. He had never seen cruelty and suffering administered and received so casually. But now he saw his opportunity. Cerberus was still glaring at his hounds and his back was turned.

Dashing between them he raced down the road. Hearing their cries close behind he forced himself to run harder. Ahead of him lay the Temple and he knew places to hide. Incredibly though, fingers dug into his heel and pulled him down.

"My father told me you were fast," Cerberus panted. "But I have been training for the sprints since I could walk. I expected a better test. You could not have thought I would ever turn my back on a prisoner." Between deep breaths he laughed.

Maybe so, thought Dip. Except you are the one who is short of breath.

Jackal and Wolf caught up to them and Dip again was hauled to his feet, this time his arms were held by the larger and heavier Jackal.

"What is your name, and what city are you from?" Cerberus said.

Dip looked at the temple, it's normally gleaming marble columns were dulled by overcast skies.

"My name is Dip and I, I have no city."

"No city! Then you are beneath even the helots. At least they belong to Sparta."

Dip could not hold back the tears. He had no home. He tried to keep his head down, but Cerberus grabbed him by the hair and forced his face up to the sky.

"We have nothing to fear from this one."

Just then, the sun broke through the clouds. Its light was so brilliant that Cerberus put up his hand to shield his eyes, releasing Dip in the process. Dip kept his face turned upwards and the warmth of the sun's rays dried his tears.

"Beware of the sun," Dip whispered into Cerberus' ear. "Apollo will protect me."

Cerberus backed away and Dip was immediately seized again and led past the temple, down into the streets of Delphi. Shopkeepers in the agora were busy organising their stalls, anticipating the crowds' return at the conclusion of the day's competition. Dip recognised several of the merchants and he tried to meet their eyes with his own, but when they saw the company of Spartans escorting him they busied themselves, pretending to take no notice. Except for one.

He was burly, average in height. Many times Dip had run past his stand while the fishseller, Pontus, unloaded basket after basket of fish from the fishermen's carts. Dip knew him for his easy smile. Now his face bore a scowl aimed at Dip's escort.

Leaning over the edge of his cart he flicked an apronful of scales in the direction of the Spartans. The three Spartans jumped and twisted, cursing as they avoided the slimy shower.

"I see it takes three bullies to guard one boy," Pontus said. "Only Spartans need numbers like this to win their battles. Then again, I expected as much from your kind. Of course you can correct me if I'm wrong."

Cerberus marched to the front of the fishseller's stall, hand on the hilt of his sword. However he quickly covered his nose and mouth as Pontus slammed a full bucket of eels down on the counter.

"Peasant," Cerberus said. "Come out from behind this stink and face me."

Pontus came around to the front of his stand. His tunic, stained with blood and caked with dried scales, was open at the front, revealing a sea serpent tattoo. He held a squirming eel, its jaws propped apart by sharpened sticks. Cerberus flinched and pulled back.

Knocking the wooden splinters from the eel's mouth, the shopkeeper threw it at the Spartans, who scrambled out of the way.

Rolling and snapping, the eel bounced around until Jackal skewered it and flung it to the side.

Cerberus drew his sword and advanced towards the fishseller.

"We Spartans are superior to all others. Peasant, I demand an apology."

Pontus inhaled deeply and laughed. High-pitched and loud, it reverberated throughout the marketplace.

Cerberus' face turned red. "How dare you! My father is a general. No one has ever shown such disrespect. Stop it. Stop it now. Do as I say or I will run you through."

The fishseller quieted. "That would be a mistake. I am not a peasant. My name is Pontus and you have much to learn about challenging men instead of children."

Lightening quick, Pontus grabbed Cerberus' sword by the hilt, pinned his arms, and lay the edge within finger's breadth of the Spartan's throat. Jackal and Wolf drew their swords, waiting for some word or gesture from their leader.

Pontus laughed again. "Boys pretending to be men. Fortunately for you I only fight men."

A roar could be heard in the distance.

"I hear another champion being crowned," he said. "The market will soon be full and I must finish organising my stall. Don't worry, I will not harm you."

Pontus relaxed his hold and Cerberus rolled away, quickly surrounded by his hounds.

"The sword I will keep as a remembrance of this meeting. As I said though, I do not fight boys. Now, off with you."

Muttering to himself, Cerberus ripped Wolf's sword from his hands and led them away. Dip's heart sank.

"What about me?"

Pontus sighed. "I told you I will not fight children, even young Spartan warriors. There is one though."

His words were lost amidst a hubbub of voices. The spectators were returning from the stadium.

"What?" Dip yelled.

"Silence," said Cerberus. "That peasant will not fight us. There is nothing he can do."

"Maybe not," added a new voice. "But I think he was trying to tell you there is much I can do."

The Spartans stopped and stared. Standing in the path in front of them with sword drawn was a slight figured warrior in full armour.

CHAPTER FIVE

Bronze armour covered much of the warrior's body. Foot armour riveted to the sandals stretched to the knees. A breastplate encircled the torso. The helmet, lined with leather and topped with a plume of white horse hair, reached to the back of the neck, and a long nosepiece attached to its front left only the eyes, mouth and jaw exposed. Arms, shoulders and thighs were free of any coverings. In the warrior's right hand was a double-edged sword. The left held a round shield, which bore no mark or emblem.

It would have been difficult to tell the warrior was a girl had it not been for the tight, black curls spilling out from under her helmet and the sound of her voice as she challenged the Spartans.

"Let him go or taste your own blood."

"Cassandra," Dip said.

"A girl," said Cerberus. "A girl dares to challenge us. I am not a child playing at being a warrior. My fifteenth year began two days ago. I was renamed Cerberus, and in celebration I tattooed my namesake myself."

He sucked in his breath, then grinned and pulled back the sleeve of his right arm. A three headed dog baring blood-tipped fangs decorated his forearm. The skin surrounding the tattoo was pink and puffy.

Reaching down, he then lifted his tunic up to his thigh and traced his finger across a double set of teeth marks that pushed his skin up like tiny protruding volcanoes.

"In my seventh year I stole a fox. It was from my uncle's private collection. He caught me climbing out of the pen and I hid the fox beneath my tunic. It writhed against my chest, slid down to my waist and sunk its teeth into my flesh. I did not cry out. My father would have been proud if he had known, but I never confessed."

Grinding and pressing his knuckles together, Cerberus continued. "My first triumph occurred at age five. I had a brother. My father decided that he was not fit to be a Spartan warrior and allowed me to take him high up the mountain. He was only two days old but I was not saddened. He would not have become a soldier."

Cerberus spread his feet shoulder width apart and held his sword in front of him with both hands.

"Girl, I do not know why you are challenging us and I do not care. My name is Cerberus and these are my hounds. We are going to send your soul straight to Hades."

A slow menacing growl pierced his teeth and Wolf and Jackal flanked his sides. Interlocking their shields with his, they formed a wall of tangled snakes and fangs and in unison they advanced, one step at a time.

Cassandra looked up to the sky, lifted her sword high

above her head and pointed it towards the sun. A golden ray burst onto its shaft and flung itself into Cerberus' eyes. Startled, he dropped his sword; blinded and swearing he fumbled for it, knocking his hounds down. Skirting the fallen Spartans, Dip ran to Cassandra's side.

"Hounds," Cerberus said, "don't wait for me. Get them now."

Jackal and Wolf started towards them, yipping.

Cassandra pushed Dip towards Wolf.

"Leave the big one to me. You look after the smallest, he has no sword and only one arm. That shouldn't be a problem."

Easy for you to say, Dip thought. He had never been in a fight and even a one-armed weaponless Spartan warrior seemed a formidable opponent. Where was he?

Growls came from behind his left ear. Pivoting on his right foot he ducked and rolled, then scrambled to his feet.

Four paces away, Wolf glared at him, his tongue sliding around his mouth, one arm limp at his side. He had discarded his shield in favour of a slim dagger, which he held straight out at arm's length towards Dip.

"You are a quick coward," Wolf said.

"Force him towards me." Cerberus, although still sightless, had drawn Wolf's sword. I'll fix him so he can't flee."

Cerberus swung his sword in a wide arc. It came within an arm's length of Dip and ripped through a thin, wooden support for a stand piled high with pomegranates. They spilled on the ground around Dip's feet. He grabbed one particularly ripe fruit and threw it at Cerberus. It hit him squarely on the back of his head and the dark red juice ran down Cerberus' neck and underneath his tunic.

Infuriated, Cerberus charged ahead, swinging his sword wildly. Unable to see, he could not tell where Dip was.

"Watch out sir," Wolf said.

"Leave me be, I can see him."

It was too late. Cerberus crashed into a pile of melons stacked waist high.

"Now I have you." Cerberus plunged his sword deep into the heart of one especially large melon.

Wolf rushed to his side.

"No Sir, these are just fruit. Our enemy is over there."

Cerberus paid no attention, continuing to stab at the melon until nothing remained except pulp, which flew through the air covering both boys. Wiping seeds and juice from his face, Cerberus felt around until he found Wolf, and grabbing his good arm he twisted it until the boy squealed in pain.

"Don't you ever correct me again. Is that understood!"

"Yes sir."

"Now find that boy and hold him until I get there."

"Right away sir."

While Cerberus and Wolf were tangled in the melons, Dip spotted Cassandra in a corner of the market engaged in a fierce battle with Jackal. She was parrying blows with such speed that her sword was a blur.

People filled the square and a group quickly formed around the two fighters, hiding them from Dip's view. He heard choruses of "move to the left," "thrust right," and then a yelp of pain. Jackal staggered out from the circle of spectators, blood pouring from a gash at his elbow. Cheering broke out, the crowd separated, and Cassandra stepped through, her sword held high.

"Well done Cassandra," Dip said as he waved at her.

Cassandra waved back swinging her sword in broad circles above her head, causing a few people around her to duck.

She certainly seems to have a lot of energy left, Dip thought. Then he heard the growling again. Out of the corner of his eye he saw a burst of light coming at him. Ducking and spinning low to the ground, he swept his legs in a circle. His feet hit Wolf's ankles, knocking him down and the dagger flew off to the side. Dip pounced onto Wolf's chest, pinning him to the ground.

He smiled down at Wolf. "I thought Spartans were tough."

Of course it did help that one of Wolf's shoulders was hanging out of its socket and the other arm was terribly twisted. Still, a Spartan was a Spartan.

"Finish me," Wolf said. "I cannot endure this humiliation."

By this time a few people gathered around them.

"Yes, do it," they urged.

Dip shivered. Winning a fight was one thing. Actually killing another person was not what he expected.

"Here, you can use this."

It was Pontus, something was hidden behind his back.

Not Cerberus's sword, Dip thought. "Pontus, I can't do this."

But instead of handing Dip a sword, Pontus tossed him the dead eel.

"An eel? What am I supposed to do with this?"

Slime and bits of flaking skin coated his hands as he tossed the eel back and forth. Wolf violently swung his head from side to side, trying to avoid the blood and grease dropping from the deteriorating body. A few scales fell into his mouth and he choked and spit them back up at Dip, who grinned. He now knew what to do.

Wolf started to speak but didn't get to utter a sound. With a quick thrust, Dip shoved the eel headfirst into the Spartan's mouth. It was the final disgrace. Dip rolled off of Wolf, who, with both arms dangling at his side, dove into the pile of melons, only the tail visible between his teeth.

Thunder reverberated throughout the market and raindrops fell. At the same time the crowd emptied, leaving Dip, Cassandra and Cerberus standing alone. Cerberus stopped rubbing his eyes and glared at Cassandra.

"I don't know how you defeated my hounds but I will have to deal with you later. This temple rat belongs to my father."

Cassandra stepped between them.

"That won't be possible," she said.

Across the square Dip saw Pontus waving them over. He was pointing at figures emerging from the shadows at the far end of the market.

"Come on Cassandra, we have to make a run for it."

Cassandra nodded.

"Another time Cerberus," she said, hurling her sword at the Spartan, who lost his footing as he ducked. They took off towards Pontus, who had the entrance to a side street blocked off with his cart. Behind them Dip heard Cerberus' roar. Side by side they ran and just as Pontus reached to pull them clear, Cassandra, in her armour and tired from her battle with Jackal, stumbled and fell. Cerberus was on her with his sword at her throat before Dip had time to react.

"No," Dip said. "Leave her alone. It's me you want."

He tried to move closer but Pontus hauled him over the barricade.

Cerberus' black eyes glowed as he stared down at Cassandra. "The rat I will deal with later. This is for the trouble you have caused me."

Cassandra tried to squirm out from under him, but using the hilt of his sword, Cerberus viciously drove the butt end into the side of her head, knocking her helmet off. Then he raised his sword, tip poised.

Dip struggled to cross the barricade, but Pontus held him firm.

"Don't worry," Cassandra said. "I am not afraid."

Raising a hand she caressed Cerberus' cheek. Her arm did not quiver.

"I didn't realise," he said. "Who are you?"

"Release me," said Cassandra, and Cerberus rose, dropping his sword.

Cassandra leapt to her feet and much to Dip's surprise put her arms around Cerberus and kissed him. Dashing to the fish cart she vaulted high over its edge to safety.

"What was that all about?" Dip said.

"I'm not sure. It just seemed like the right thing to do. And it worked, he's leaving."

Cerberus was walking to the far end of the marketplace where Hades and Pantheras stood waiting.

"No wonder all the people left," Dip said. "I would not want to be cheering on the defeat of a Spartan with those two around."

Jackal crawled out from under a pottery stand and joined Cerberus. Wolf came out from behind the pile of melons, the fish still lodged in his mouth. Pantheras ripped it out. Wolf, choking and sputtering, fell to his knees. Jackal also dropped to his knees, bowing his head before the Spartan General. Only Cerberus remained standing, his back straight, defiant.

Dip could not hear what was being said but Hades' tone was unmistakably harsh. Cerberus made no move, he seemed quite calm. Too calm, apparently, for his father. With a suddenness that startled Dip, Hades brought his hand up and struck his son in the face. The force of the blow knocked Cerberus to his knees. Bleeding from the mouth, Cerberus continued to stare at his father. Hades put his face close to his son's then straightened, grabbed Cerberus's arm and forced him face first into the street. A trickle of water from the rain streamed past his face.

Jackal pointed in their direction. Hades jerked his son up and shoved him forward.

Dip turned to Pontus to thank him but the fishseller cut

him off with a wave of his hand and fled down an alley.

"Help me take this armour off," Cassandra said. "Believe me, we don't want to be caught by the Spartans now. Cerberus is getting exactly what he deserves."

But as she said it, her voice broke and Dip could see tears in her eyes as she ran down the sidestreet. He turned and ran after her.

CHAPTER SIX

After a few blocks of running, Dip and Cassandra once again encountered numbers of people wandering through the street and they felt safe enough to stop and mingle with the crowds. Dip pulled Cassandra to an empty doorway and sat her down on the step beside him.

"I thought you hated Spartans. Why did you kiss him?"

Cassandra grabbed Dip's wrist and twisted his arm easily behind his back. "Don't you go accusing me of anything. I saved your spine, that is if you have any."

"You're hurting me Cassandra!"

Giving one final twist, Cassandra bounced Dip into the corner of the doorway and put her knee on his chest.

"Just count yourself lucky Pontus is an escaped Helot too. There is a network of us set up throughout Greece. Pontus was responsible for gathering weapons for those of us here. Where do you think I have been spending my time the past few months? Not running aimlessly around the countryside like you. I've been training with him since I arrived. In the future no one will be able to challenge or frighten me."

Especially when your knees are cutting off someone's air, Dip thought.

"When you foolishly ran down to the stadium I spotted Cerberus and his hounds closing in on you. There wasn't time then to warn you and I knew the path back to their camp would take them through the market. I found Pontus, told him the Spartans were after you and had him delay Cerberus while I put on my armour."

"Did you tell him about the oracle?" Dip could barely speak.

"No, there wasn't time. Anyways Pontus was eager to help. He thinks of Spartans the same way I do."

Cassandra rolled off Dip and poked him in the chest. "And don't you forget it."

Brushing Cassandra's hand away, Dip drew his knees up under his chin. "Wasn't I at least a little heroic in the market?"

"I will never forget seeing Wolf run with that eel in his mouth," she laughed, leaning over and giving Dip a quick hug. "I suppose you are showing some signs of being a hero. Maybe I should call you my little Heracles instead of temple rat. Do you wish to run with the gods as well? If you do," she squeezed Dip's upper arm, "perhaps some muscles would help."

"Don't mock me," Dip replied getting to his feet. He had once confided to Cassandra his admiration of Heracles' strength and stamina. "I may not have Heracles' muscles, but at least I have his integrity. And up until now I thought yours was beyond question. Why didn't Cerberus strike you?"

Cassandra stopped laughing and faced Dip. She was slightly taller and now she held herself even higher.

"That's one question I cannot answer. I was certain he was going to kill me and I was praying to Apollo. Then a kind of serenity came over me and I think Cerberus felt it as well. He stopped and it was over."

"Not quite."

This time it was Cassandra's turn to blush.

"I suppose that kiss was also Apollo's will," Dip said.

"Never mind about that." Cassandra grabbed Dip by the tunic, drew him close, then shoved him aside. "Let's just concentrate on your problem."

Cassandra turned to leave but her path was blocked by a man coming out of a nearby doorway. Swaying, he staggered down the street singing an ode to Apollo, carrying a large wineskin that splashed thick purple drops with every step. Stumbling against the curb, the wineskin fell from his grasp, bouncing onto the dirt, its contents spilling and mixing with the slippery soil.

Interrupting his ode, he turned his face to the sky and sighed. "I hope the aroma satisfies you Apollo. You cannot appreciate it's fullness of flavour like us mortals, but take me at my word," and he winked at Dip, "as usual."

"Barbarian," Cassandra said. "Nobody except foolish drunkards drink undiluted wine."

"To Apollo and glorious victory," he shouted, raising the wineskin once again, letting the few remaining drops wet his lips as he lay down in front of Dip.

"Come on Cassandra," Dip said. "Apollo reviles drunkenness

as any fool should know. Heracles was not beyond the odd sip, but his wine was always diluted. Except of course, after pursuing the Cerynean Stag for an entire year. That would have given anyone a powerful thirst. I mean what was a hero to do?"

Cassandra rolled her eyes and shook her head.

"Please Dip, give Heracles and The Labours a rest for now."

"The Labours!" The man sat up so suddenly Dip had to leap quickly out of the way to avoid being dumped into the street himself. Dripping mud, he put his hand over his heart and started to speak.

"Allow me to introduce myself. My name is Free Poet Stratus, in demand throughout Greece. I pride myself on my knowledge of the gods, however I have never heard The Labours recited as fully and eloquently as I have tonight. How beautiful were the lyrics. I cried when the boy told of Heracles finally ascending through the clouds to Olympus. If you enjoy tales of the gods and it seems fewer do, you should have been there."

Stratus burped loudly, shrugged his shoulders at the empty wineskin and tossed it aside. "To Heracles and our new champion, may he reign supreme forever."

Cassandra shook her head disgustedly and began to move away but Dip stopped her. He addressed the poet.

"Did you say a boy was reciting The Labours?"

"Yes and a fine job he was doing too. A pity I had to leave, but my wineskin was almost empty and I left to find some more. Say you wouldn't happen to know of a fine establishment eager to hear my tales?"

Dip cut him off. "This boy, was his left arm withered, useless?"

"Could have been, one arm always seemed to be behind his back. Of course it could have been an affectation designed to gain sympathy even though he didn't need it. His knowledge of The Labours for one so young was quite remarkable. He even called himself 'Odysseus,' a stage name I suppose, the crowd loved him."

"I knew it," Dip said. "He's our companion and we need to find him at once."

"Show us where he is." This time Cassandra poked her finger in the poet's chest.

"A wonderful idea considering my, ah, particular needs at this moment. A return trip to the banquet is in order. Friends of Odysseus you say."

Cocking his head to one side he rubbed his lower lip between his thumb and forefinger.

"Would this have anything to do with the skirmish I just heard about? It is being told that two fierce warriors, one unarmed, sent three young Spartans scampering out of the square with their tails between their legs. That would have been something to see. Some are even saying one was a young female."

Stratus spun to his feet.

"It doesn't matter. Any friend of Odysseus will be welcome at our celebration. It isn't often that Athens can celebrate Sparta being defeated on two occasions in one night. After all, our sprinter did beat the Spartan champion."

"You're an Athenian! Then you are just the person I'm

looking for," Dip said. "I have an important message for your city."

Stratus laughed. "I'm sure you do young one, but I'm not Athenian myself, only a poor yet respected poet who happens to be in their company for the games. I've found it helps to refer to myself as citizen to the city employing me, keeps the wine flowing you know. I know someone at the banquet you can talk to and I'm sure your friend will be happy to see you."

Stratus headed down the street. "Come on, it's not far."

"I hope so," Cassandra said to Dip. "I just saw Jackal. The others can't be far behind."

CHAPTER SEVEN

All three walked down the street, Stratus in the lead weaving slightly with Dip and Cassandra pushing him along. They passed several rows of houses, each separated by a narrow alley and built only to the second floor. Dip skirted around garbage piled in small heaps, fed on silently by rats.

Stratus, although still out of balance, managed to avoid the waste, while Cassandra took a direct path, kicking and scattering the rats and their meal. A few bared their teeth but Cassandra took no notice.

They had travelled no more than a couple of blocks when the poet stopped in front of a narrow entrance leading to two large oak doors. It was a private residence belonging to one of the wealthiest men in Delphi, although you couldn't tell by the exterior. It was similar to almost all the other houses. Walls made of mud brick extended along its length and crumbled to the touch after a few years. Burglars found it easy to drill holes through different sections and Dip could see a few areas patched with clay.

Dip had never been inside but he often ran past and once

when a slave left, he caught a glimpse of colourful mosaics lining the stone floor.

Stratus raised both fists and pounded on the doors. A few seconds passed but all they could hear was loud laughter. When the noise died down the poet hammered once more, and this time they heard a heavy scrape of sandal on stone.

The doors swung open and a massive torso faced Dip. At least that was all he could see. Dip knew there was a head attached to the body but it was too high to see properly. Even Cassandra was shocked at the size of the man in front of them. Stratus was not impressed.

"Oh, Titan, it's you," he said, tapping the torso. "Don't stand there blocking our way like the giant you are, let us by."

"Master poet," Titan began. His words were slow and controlled. "I threw you out. You were not to return."

"Thrown out, you didn't tell us that," Dip said.

"I prefer to think of it as leaving on my own to freely pursue the fruits and pleasures of Dionysus."

"No, Stratus, I threw you out," said the giant.

Stratus turned to Dip and Cassandra. "This man has obviously wrestled one match too many and suffered terrible blows to the head. He does not know what he is saying."

"I was Athenian champion. I would have been victorious in the Games if I had not injured my knee in the chariot race."

"How did that happen?" Dip craned his neck upward trying for a glimpse of Titan's face. A mass of beard protruded over a muscled chest.

"Titan thought he could beat the other charioteers more easily if he pulled the chariot himself," Stratus said.

"Yes, and I would have won too if not for the hole I stepped in."

Titan straightened himself even higher and laughed. It boomed over Dip and Cassandra causing them to cover their ears.

"That was a good race."

"Now tell them what happened to you after the race."

Titan's chuckles stopped. "I could not wrestle with my injury and my sponsors left me. You helped me Stratus."

"Yes. When Athens abandoned you I took care of you like you were my own, and this is how you repay me, by throwing me out of the victory celebration I was supposed to be in service for."

"You were drinking too much."

"I stopped didn't I?"

"Yes, only after I threw you out."

Dip continued to stare alternately up at Titan and then at Stratus, but Cassandra couldn't stand it anymore. She kicked both of them in the shins. Stratus fell to the ground in pain while Titan, as if studying a new born puppy, stroked Cassandra's hair. His eyes were deep brown, gentle and alive.

"What would you like little one?"

"Please let us in, there are Spartans after us and we need to see our friend Odysseus."

Titan lifted Cassandra up from under her arms and held her at eye level.

"You should have said so earlier. Of course I will allow

you in. I love a good story and he entertains me. Not like this one." He put Cassandra down and gestured at Stratus, who moaned and held his leg to his chest. "All right, you can come in as well, only this time I will pour your wine."

Titan led them through an open courtyard. Dip paused to look at the mosaics lining the floor, running his hand over the hundreds of fitted tiles, some no bigger than his fingernail. Images of the gods stared at him and he averted his eyes. As they rounded a corner they could see the main room ahead of them. A purple curtain closed it off and the murmur of a crowd came from inside. Dip was distracted by a mosaic beside the entrance.

"Cassandra, come look at this one," Dip said.

It was the largest and most spectacular mosaic yet.

"Everyone has been struck by it," Stratus said. "Apollo's temple has been faithfully recreated wouldn't you say? Hold on, I haven't noticed Heracles in this one before."

Dip pressed his face close to a group of four darker tiles set in amongst the clouds. A dark, muscular figure clothed in a lionskin stretched his arms up to the heavens. He ran his hand over the four tiles and to his horror they fell at his feet.

Stratus knitted his brow as Dip tried to replace them. "Looks like someone has been practising some amateur craftsmanship. I'm sure our host won't be happy about this. No matter, you might as well keep them. Perhaps they'll bring you luck."

Suddenly the front doors shook as if struck by a battering ram.

"Of course," Stratus said, slipping through the curtain, "I've been wrong before."

"I'll hold the Spartans off," Titan said. "You get your friend."

CHAPTER EIGHT

Dip and Cassandra followed Stratus through the purple curtain and entered a small, square chamber. Tables laden with spiced boar haunches, pheasant necks, black blood pudding, and innumerable currants, olives and roasted nuts, lined the walls.

Dip's stomach roared. At the temple the priestess always provided him with the basics; potatoes, bread, goat, and at times he scrounged odds and ends at the market. A feast like this was almost incomprehensible.

Slaves, balding and somewhat rotund from lives of valued service, were busy filling plates, rushing off through another doorway. Dip couldn't help it. Sidling around to the edge of a table he smiled at one of the slaves, slipped a piece of boar into his mouth and shaking slightly, wiped the juice from his chin.

"Hey, save your stomach for later."

Cassandra dug her elbow into his side, but she winked at him and Dip noted she was chewing something too.

"This way," said Stratus, and he opened the next purple

curtain and ushered them through into a huge banquet room filled with Athenian men. Except for the slaves scurrying around, everyone reclined on couches; most were eating or having their plates and cups filled by the always attentive slaves. Propped up by pillows, the Athenians rested on their left elbows. With their free hands they ate their food which had been cut up by the slaves and set out on small tables in front of them.

The Athenians were too busy eating and drinking to notice their arrival. Small groups were being entertained by different performers. Several girls danced rhythmically swinging fine pieces of shimmering drapery that revealed various bits of their anatomy. A juggler intermittently balanced knives on the tip of his nose, drawing loud cheers from the far end of the room and a flute player struggled to be heard in front of another group.

A bright-eyed boy of about seven years sat on the floor in the centre of the room eating from a bowl. Or rather, attacking his food, ripping pieces of meat off a boar's leg with gusto. He used only his right arm. His left, half hidden in the folds of his oversized, grimy tunic, was motionless. Seeing Dip, he waved and bobbed his soil encrusted hair, particles of dirt drifting into the air, reflecting in the sunlight.

Stratus pulled Cassandra and Dip down beside him. "You'll have to wait until the entertainers have finished, otherwise it would be terribly rude. Your friend is a likeable little fellow. I tried to talk to him, but it was very hard. The dust kept me sneezing"

Dip nodded. "I've tried to bathe him," he said. "It's all I can do to make sure his face is wiped clean. He won't let me touch his hair."

Stratus furrowed his brow and started to speak but Dip cut him off.

"He says it's who he is. The family he lived with kept him bald, like he was a slave. After he left them he let his hair grow and now refuses to even wash it. If people don't know his name they ask for the clay-haired boy."

"What do you mean?" Stratus said.

"Odysseus is like you. He recites heroic stories and poems for his supper. He stands on a corner repeating passages until someone tosses him some coins, or he hears of a banquet or gathering and winds his way in among the other entertainers. But as he speaks of the heroes and gods, he transforms, as if the gods not only walk beside him, but whisper in his ear. It's quite mesmerizing. By night's end he stays on as a guest of his host or he makes his way to the temple where I look after him. Now I don't know what will happen. I don't even know where my home will be."

"Yes, your friend is one odd outcast," Cassandra said.

Dip glared at her. "How would you know Cassandra, you've ignored him since you arrived here. He has no parents either, just like us. For some reason the Oracle put us all in this together and you better learn that Odysseus is just as important as you and I, even if he is a little different."

Cassandra's eyes flashed and she raised her arm as if to strike, but stopped as suddenly as she started and put her hands into her lap.

"I'm sorry Dip. After what happened to my parents and my brother, accepting others is still hard, but I'm changing."

"My, my," Stratus said. "This is all quite intriguing. Now we have the Oracle involved. I am beginning to think I may have underestimated your importance. You mentioned something about a message for the Athenians. I believe the person you want to talk to is right over there."

The poet pointed to a man in a grey tunic reclined on a couch near the front of the room. His beard stood out in contrast to the beardless Athenians and slaves around him.

"It's the general from the stadium," Dip said. "Can you arrange a meeting for me Stratus?"

"I don't see why not. After all, Miltiades did hire my services for this party. Wait here."

Stratus stepped around several couches until he was by the general's side. Dip saw him point in their direction and the Athenian smiled and began to laugh.

"This is it Cassandra. You and Odysseus have led me to the Athenians. I'm about to fulfil the oracle."

Dip tried to rise. A large hand held him down.

"You must be careful," said Titan. "I could not refuse the Spartans entrance any longer. All are welcome at an Athenian banquet."

Dip spun around and peered through Titan's legs. At the entrance to the room were two fully armed Spartans. They hid behind Titan as Hades and his aide entered. Following close behind, carefully scanning the room, were Cerberus and his hounds.

CHAPTER NINE

The Spartan guard moved aside and Pantheras stepped forward.

"All bow, prostrate yourself in the presence of Lord Hades, master of Sparta, master of the Underworld."

Conversations were cut off in mid-breath, all was still. Then muted laughter echoed from the centre of the room. Knocking over couches and scattering slaves, Hades leaped to face the smirking Athenian general.

Dip and Cassandra, still shielded by Titan's massive legs, were joined by Odysseus and Dip put his arm around the boy's shoulders.

"Odysseus, you're shaking."

"Beware, beware." Odysseus leaned in close to Dip.

"Of what?" Dip said.

"I switched the tiles. I will show you the way, like Heracles. The answer is in your odyssey. I am Odysseus. Listen to me. The journey is perilous and the souls of the dead await you. It is the only path you can take to Hades' realm. Trust the gods. Trust me."

His voice drifted off and Dip felt the shaking subside. Odysseus held out his damaged arm to Cassandra. She took it and pressed it to her cheek as Hades' harsh tones filled the room.

"How dare you. You cheat Sparta out of victory in the games today and you mock your superior. My champion, my daughter Kheerna, should have won."

"Champion no longer," said Miltiades. "This is an Athenian celebration, Hades, or whatever you dare call yourself. We are obligated to treat you as a guest, but do not try my patience and intelligence with unfounded accusations. Unlike Sparta, we educate our young to think for themselves. The feebleminded may embrace you as a god, but don't count on supporters outside of your realm. Perhaps you should train your runners fully to deal with circumstance, rather than ignorant devotion."

"Your man deliberately caused Kheerna to stumble. Blinded her path coming from the shadow into the sunlight. Caused her injury. It was an unfair advantage."

"Unfortunately we are not that skilled. Your daughter followed too close, she needed to keep her head up and her mind active to recognize when the darkness on the track ended and the light began. Remember Hades, we are in Delphi, not Sparta. The sun's glare is most keenly felt at the top of the mountain. Perhaps you should have sought the Oracle's advice, as I did."

Hades grabbed his sidelock and began twisting it, his face flushing.

"I was never a supporter of that old hag, common

military sense is always preferable to unyielding opinion, but her death is regrettable and the Persians must be punished for their actions. In the name of Apollo of course."

"In due time Hades. There is no doubt our combined armies can easily defeat any Persian force. We both spoke our piece at the games tonight, honouring Apollo's voice and the selection process for a new oracle is already underway. It won't be long before the white smoke will signal its conclusion. From what I understand there are few candidates, your daughter among them."

Hades motioned to Pantheras, who rushed to his side and began whispering in his ear and shaking his head. Hades reached out to Pantheras' shoulder but stopped as his aide shrank away.

"Calm yourself Hades. I have no spies in your camp."

Miltiades waved his hand and a slave set a cup of wine and a bowl of currants in front of the Spartans.

"In my visit to the Oracle, she spoke vaguely, as is customary, but she did mention a successor, a girl-warrior, and I knew you had a daughter."

Hades spat on the floor in front of the Athenian general. "Did she also tell you how to cheat us out of our victory?"

"No, but since you seem so curious, I shall let you judge that part of the priestess' prophecy for yourself. My poet accompanied me. He can repeat the oracle to you."

Miltiades reached back and pulled Stratus to the front of the couch. The poet reached for the wine left for Hades and drank, using both hands to steady the cup.

Bowing to both generals, he began tapping the side of his head.

"What is he doing?" Hades said.

"Merely an affectation," Miltiades replied. "He is well paid and quite eloquent in his own fashion."

"Yes." Stratus beamed. "This tapping is an art form unto itself. It soothes and stimulates the brain, increasing interlobular appreciation and verbosity."

"Enough," said Hades. "It's giving me a headache."

Knocking Stratus' hand away, Hades pinned it to the table and drew his sword.

"One warning only, poet. Next time you will not have any fingers left with which to torment me."

Stratus reclaimed his hand, forced it down to his side and cleared his throat while Miltiades suppressed a laugh and nodded.

"This was the oracle as I heard it."

'Miltiades, the fate of your runner is in my hands. He will run a long and arduous race to test his courage against Apollo. Athens must learn from his victory. Look to a youth and reward him well.'

Miltiades rose from the couch and stepped to within an arm's length of the Spartan general. Cerberus ran to his father's side.

"My aides assured me it meant an Athenian victory in the games. One does not question an oracle but they have a history of being open to interpretation. I'm glad you barged in on our celebration, Hades, because I too believe today's race was inconclusive. Its outcome cannot be changed but I believe it was not the race the Oracle was talking about. I believe the Oracle's prophecy talked of a race with Apollo, taking endurance, stamina, and true courage. All qualities found in a hero."

"Like Heracles," Stratus interrupted.

"Yes, like Heracles. Today's sprint would not have measured this. Athens will sponsor a new contest and I declare this to be Apollo's Race. The Oracle meant for this race to be contested by youths and the winner will have to run the mountain. As well, the victor must complete the course before Apollo finishes his journey across the sky in his chariot. Here at Delphi, the winner must race Apollo for his victory. I will personally crown the champion with a garland of laurel leaves."

An excited murmur ran through the banquet hall. Hades bent and whispered to his son. After a few seconds the room quieted and Hades addressed Miltiades.

"Athenian, Sparta will accept your challenge. We relish the opportunity to humiliate any youth foolish enough to race against a Spartan. Indeed, my own son Cerberus will represent Sparta. Be prepared to bow down to him as you place the victory wreath upon his head."

"Apollo's Race will be open to any who wish to compete. Your son? I hope he runs better than he fights. Events earlier today in the market have been the subject of much merriment."

Cerberus howled and charged Miltiades. "Go for your sword. I'll show you how I fight."

Dip felt Titan's leap and the three youths dove out of his way. The giant reached Miltiades just in time to intercept Cerberus' thrust and knock him aside. Hades' bodyguard charged, but Titan, with his feet in a practised wrestler's stance, deflected their blows easily and threw them to the ground.

Hades lunged at Miltiades, but Titan was able to throw out a foot and trip him. Several portly Athenian politicians panicked and made for the doorway, knocking aside several couches and tables. Currants slid across the floor underneath Hades and his bodyguard, causing them to cartwheel as they tried to get up. Even Titan skidded across the room only stopping by grabbing onto a chandelier.

Dignitaries and guests ran past Dip and Cassandra, blocking their view. Dip felt a familiar hand on his shoulder and he struggled beneath Cerberus' grip. He dug his elbow into the Spartan's side. It was like hitting a rock.

Cassandra drew her dagger but Jackal held her arms from behind. Bending at the waist, Cassandra flipped him over her back and he crashed into Dip and Cerberus, knocking them down.

"Prepare to meet Hades," Cerberus growled, raising his sword.

Dip closed his eyes, but instead of feeling sword against his flesh, he heard Cassandra's laugh and he looked around. All he could see were the bottoms of the two Spartans' sandals. Titan had hoisted each by their tunics high overhead.

"Enough," Miltiades shouted. "Titan, put them down."

He pulled the Spartan general to his feet.

"You have overstayed your welcome. Collect your son and leave."

Cerberus and Jackal sheathed their swords and turned to Dip and Cassandra.

"This isn't over yet," Cerberus said. "A good soldier always has an alternate battle plan. Look to the doorway. As you can see, Wolf has your young friend. If you want him to survive, meet me at the stadium when the night is darkest. Don't be late."

Pushing past Titan, they jostled several others as they joined Wolf and dragged Odysseus out of the room.

CHAPTER TEN

Cassandra pounded her fist into her palm. "We need to save Odysseus and we must find out more information about this race. If you win then you can tell the Athenians about the oracle. There isn't much time, we can surprise the Spartans before they reach the stadium."

She reached for Dip's arm but he pulled away. "No, not now. Cerberus said when the night was darkest. I think we should just go to the temple and wait. I, I mean, we will be safe there."

"Look, unlike you, I do not fear a battle with any Spartan, but I can wait until the appointed time. You go hide like a temple rat. I'll meet you there later."

Brushing past Dip, she joined the crowd on the banquet floor. Dip put his hand to his heart.

Maybe he wasn't courageous like Heracles, but it wasn't his fault. The temple was his home, he had to go there.

It was only a short distance, but to Dip it seemed longer than any run he had been on. Reaching the entrance, with one hand on his heart he backed up the temple steps, peered around a column and waited as the sun slowly began to set.

Finally, through the fading daylight, he could see Cassandra striding towards him. Flashes of bronze gleamed in her hand.

"Cassandra, over here. Come on, I know a place where we can talk. You'll have to put down your knife though. Apollo's temple is not a place for weapons."

"Temples in Sparta were not sanctuaries for us, I'll only sheath it."

A rat scurried across the floor and Cassandra jumped. Dip took her hand but she shook it free.

"I'm not afraid. It's just that I'm feeling odd vibrations from everything."

Dip led Cassandra into an antechamber, stopping briefly to say a prayer at a slender marble statue of a young woman, her face bowed.

"Nike." She bowed her head. "Victory."

Sitting on the statue's base, she looked around and breathed deeply.

"This temple calms me, Dip. I should have come here before."

"You had your reasons Cassandra. The death of your parents and the loss of your brother. Your escape from Sparta, training for battle. Now that you're here though let's make the best of our circumstance."

"Shh." Cassandra clamped her hand over Dip's mouth. Voices echoed down the corridor. "Is there a fast way out of here? Quickly!"

Dip leapt to his feet, sprinted to the far end of the

chamber and stopped at a crack in wall. Gripping the edge, he swung the crack open until there was space large enough to wriggle through. Cassandra squeezed by first and Dip followed, closing the wall behind him.

"The priestess showed this to me after I arrived. The opening was created by a great earthquake, a thousand years ago. Artisans hinged the marble for a secret door for the attendants. All I add now and then is a little animal fat to keep it greased."

Cassandra wasn't listening. She was staring through the crack at a trio of priests entering the antechamber. They also stopped at Nike's statue and offered muted prayers, their red robes contrasting vividly with the black veins running through the white marble.

Dip strained at the crack, pressing close to Cassandra. Inhaling deeply, he was overcome by her scent, a sweet fragrance that filled his lungs and delighted his heart. He moved in closer.

"Stop pushing me Dip," Cassandra said, digging her elbow into his side. "It's difficult enough hearing without you hovering."

"I just wanted, I mean I thought. Oh, never mind." Dip sat and rubbed his ribs. "What are they saying, Cassandra?"

"It's the selection team for the new priestess. They're talking about the candidates. All the usual requirements: dedication, observance, sanctity, and faith."

She shook her head. "I've heard the stories, the corruption, influence and power. You must know Dip, the priestess was your protector."

"I won't deny it," Dip said. "But she was also my friend as well as Oracle, and when she talked to me about the gods she became different. Her eyes, her tone of voice, there was none of the theatrics she showed on the tripod. Do you doubt my oracle now? Was that imagined?"

Cassandra leaned over and pressed her lips to Dip's forehead. "No, it wasn't. I felt it back on the road and being here makes me certain of it. I've always had faith, Dip, but in myself more than the gods, and certainly not in those three."

Dip pulled her away from the crack and started down a short passageway. Cassandra hesitated, then followed. They emerged onto a small ledge, stairs led down to a large chamber and at one end lay another set of stairs leading to the back of a platform encircled by transparent curtains.

"This is, I mean was, my favoured spot. We're directly behind the Oracle's chamber. From here I could observe and learn. 'Part of my education,' the priestess told me. Come on, there's another exit over here, if we're quiet we can leave without being seen."

But Cassandra was already headed towards the platform. Her eyes fixed on the tripod, she walked up the steps through the veil and sat down. The platform had been cleansed of blood but the remains of the omphalos, fine bits of splintered rock, still crunched beneath her sandals. Cassandra picked up as many as she could and ran her fingers over them.

She began to sway rhythmically, rocking and moaning and sweat rolled down her forehead.

"Power lies in this chamber, Dip, prophecies made here will still affect Spartans and Athenians, even us Helots. I can feel it."

Lines creased her forehead and she closed her eyes and strained against an invisible barrier. He reached for her arm but before he made contact she wrapped her fingers around his wrist with a ferocity that made him cry out in pain.

"Don't let me go," she whispered.

Locked in her grasp he noticed a familiar, pungent aroma wafting into the room. Prying her hand free, he interlocked his fingers with hers and pulled. She didn't budge. The aroma intensified, almost smothering him and it reached Cassandra as well, snapping her head back.

"Cassandra, we have to hide," he said, pulling her off the tripod. Clearing her eyes, Cassandra nodded, and Dip led her back to the ledge.

Three priests entered the room and stepped to the priestess' chamber. The smallest motioned to three figures obscured by the shadows at the doorway.

"Come in, come in, my Lord. We are alone. Nothing is left in here except dust, and the tripod of course. Pity the Persians destroyed the omphalos though."

"Haven't you replaced it yet?" Hades strode up the steps to the top of the chamber. "The priestess must have an egg with the strings of fate attached."

Cassandra pressed closer to Dip and this time he put his arm around her shoulders to calm her.

"Have faith. You are safe here with me." This time, he would not bolt like a scared rat.

"Lord Hades, please," continued the priest. "An egg will be carved, threads will be spun. Apollo shall be served."

Hades grabbed the priest's arm and pulled it taut. Pantheras ran from the shadows, withdrew his dagger and pressed it to the priest's throat.

"Wrong answer priest," Pantheras said. "Repeat after me, Hades shall be served."

Prostrating themselves before the Spartans, the two larger priests intoned "Hades shall be served," and it echoed throughout the chamber.

"Don't forget about me, father."

A girl dressed in flowing white robes limped up to the platform. Her red hair spilled down her back and she swept it from her face as she stared down at the fallen priests. She withdrew a small glass jar and Pantheras released the priest to rush and rub a few drops of the clear liquid onto the back of her thigh.

"If you're going to kill them, do it quickly. I've told you that this is not the place for me. I am a Spartan warrior, not some flounced and primped priestess. I should be second in command, not my fool brother."

Kheerna kicked at the tripod, knocking it over, then cursed, clutching her hamstring, while the priests struggled to right it.

"I'd thought I'd seen the last of those with the death of that weakling my mother bore. It was my duty to dispose of him, I was the eldest child. But no, my brother had to volunteer; struggling into the mountains with that three-legged monstrosity and the baby. Everyone admired him.

Now the opportunist calls himself the mighty Cerberus while I must lock myself away, sit on the accursed tripod and dress like a concubine."

Hades slumped and placed his hand on his daughter's cheek. "Forget the past, Kheerna. It was wrong. There was no need. My son was too hasty."

Kheerna slapped it away.

"Don't patronise me, father. And no more lectures on my supposed powers. First, I'm cheated out of victory in the games and now this humiliation. I belong in the field, in battle."

Sighing, Hades turned to the priests.

"You have been paid well. When the white smoke rises I expect my daughter named as Oracle. Come Pantheras."

Shaking his head he backed out of the chamber, his shoulders drooping as if carrying a great weight.

Dip and Cassandra crept down from the ledge as Kheerna continued to harangue the priests. Pressing against the wall, Dip led Cassandra from the chamber and through a maze of corridors, descending to a small antechamber containing a small wooden cot and table. Spread on the table were a few empty plates and a roughly hewn stone lamp shaped like a wild boar, mouth open, tusks broken at the base. Beside it was a slender statue of Nike. Dip picked it up and handing it to Cassandra, took a deep breath.

"It's yours Cassandra. My fate lies outside the temple.

Cassandra bowed her head. "On the tripod I had a glimpse of mine. I was surrounded by shadows and darkness. There was only one way out. I held out my hand to yours for you were the only one who could save me. Cerberus was also there, but he was no longer a threat."

Dip wanted to reach over and hug Cassandra but she seemed different, distant. "Whatever it takes Cassandra, no harm will come to you. It is the will of Apollo, part of my oracle."

"I feel the oracle too, we must save Odysseus."

Setting the statue back on the table, Cassandra picked up an empty plate. "Do you have any food around here? I fight better on a full stomach."

"This way," Dip said, taking her by the hand.

CHAPTER ELEVEN

Bits of dried goat on top of olives, weighed down by a week's supply of coarse bread sat in Dip's stomach like a rock. Movement was difficult and each step up the road to the stadium was torture. "Can't we rest, Cassandra? I feel like Heracles carrying the Erythmian Boar on his shoulders."

"You mean in your belly. I have never seen anyone eat that much. Stop complaining and keep up, we're almost there."

It was not difficult to see, even at that time of night. A full moon cast enough light for shadows to fall from the branches of nearby olive trees. Cassandra strode through them, but Dip, reminded of his meal, was careful to step over and around.

Howls broke the stillness of the night air. Cassandra withdrew her dagger and quickened her pace until they reached the stadium's entrance. The tunnel leading to the playing field was dark.

"They're waiting for us Dip. I hope you're ready. If there's any hero in you now is the time for it to come out."

Dip wasn't around. The last sprint had been too much for him. Clutching his stomach and a hand over his mouth, he raced to the nearest bush and doubled over. A few moments later he staggered back, moaning.

Cassandra put her finger to her lips and started through the tunnel. Dip followed her into the blackness. He had walked into the stadium many times when it had been deserted, imagining the crowds cheering his entrance. Now he was picking his way carefully down the darkened corridor to avoid detection. His childhood fantasies faded with each step. Coming to the end of the tunnel all were pushed from his mind.

Jackal and Wolf sat on the ground in the centre of the stadium. Between them lay Odysseus, face down, unmoving. His left arm was out to his side bent at an unnatural angle and his right hand lay on the back of his head.

Dip and Cassandra stood about halfway up the stadium. The rows of carved limestone benches spread out above and below them. The acoustics were excellent.

"We're here now," said Cassandra. "Let him go."

The two Spartans leapt up, swords in hand, dragging Odysseus to his feet.

"Come down and join us." Jackal pinned Odysseus to the ground with his knee. "But don't act hastily, your little friend is not in good shape."

Cassandra ran down, leaping three steps at a time. Dip descended slowly, turning as he went, until he too reached the playing field.

Its surface of sparse grass and gravel provided solid footing; contestants in the Games would not stumble because of uneven ground. Dip would have loved to run the length of the stadium, feel the light bounce in his stride, the strength in his legs tested against the hardness of the ground. He knew he could outrun most boys his age, but he also realised that he could not run away from the Spartans. He would have to show courage like his hero, it was time to act like Heracles.

"Hurry Dip. We can handle these two like we did in the market."

"Cassandra, stay where you are." This time it was Dip who commanded and for once Cassandra obeyed.

Odysseus' left arm hung at an odd angle from his shoulder and he was cradling it with his right arm. Dried tears shone in the moonlight against the dirt sticking to his cheeks.

"He's only a child," shouted Cassandra. "I've seen Spartan cruelty on many occasions, but only cowards and bullies hurt someone weaker and smaller than themselves."

Jackal spit and stood up. "He tried to run away. It's Hades' usual punishment."

Wolf rubbed his shoulder and took a step forward. Cassandra started to move too but Dip gripped her wrist hard and yanked her back.

"Dip, that hurts. Don't you care about Odysseus?"

"Of course I do, but remember back on the road when you asked me if I noticed anything missing from those Spartans?"

"Yes."

"Suppose you tell me what's missing now."

"There's no need for you to answer that." From the far end of the stadium, Cerberus walked out into the moonlight, dressed in armour.

At the sight of him, Cassandra ripped herself free from Dip. She set her feet shoulder length apart, dagger ready.

"No Cassandra. You're no match for Cerberus without your armour."

"It doesn't matter. This is the only way we can save Odysseus. You'll have to watch the other two while I take care of him."

She ran towards Cerberus and lunged at him. Startled at the suddenness of her attack Cerberus managed to block her blow with his shield. The impact jarred the dagger from Cassandra's hand and fell at her feet. He stepped on it.

"Wait," Cerberus said. "I'm not here to fight you."

Cassandra tilted her head slightly to the side maintaining her fighting stance.

"Perhaps you had enough of me in the market?"

"What happened in the market has been forgotten. My father should pay more attention to the gods. I understand that sometimes they do walk among us and in the marketplace it is clear you were assisted by Apollo. It does not bother me. I'm here to avenge a Spartan defeat in a different sort of battle."

Dip had had enough. He ran to Cassandra and pushed her to the side. "Just tell us how we can get our friend back. I warn you, I will not shy away from any battle either."

Cerberus took off his helmet and laughed. "What's this? Are you challenging me? Courage in the face of overwhelming danger? I would not have thought it possible when we first met. If you do walk with Apollo by your side, perhaps some of his bravado has rubbed off."

In three quick steps, Cerberus grasped the front of Dip's tunic, pulling his face close to his own. Dip tried in vain to pull away.

"I appreciate your show of bravery, but it is nighttime, and Apollo's strength only shows itself in the full light of the sun. I will deal with you soon enough. Believe me when I say mine is the face of overwhelming danger."

Cerberus laughed again, turned Dip around and barked softly behind his head as he released him. Dip stumbled and Cassandra caught him before he fell.

"Tell us what you want." Cassandra maintained her fighting stance. "If it is a fight we are ready with or without weapons."

Jackal and Wolf grinned. As they raised their swords Odysseus ran between them, not to Dip and Cassandra, but to Cerberus, who dropped his sword and gingerly lifted Odysseus' arm.

"What's this?" Cerberus turned to Jackal and Wolf, raising his sword. "What happened here?"

Odysseus pointed to the hounds. "I only ran a short distance. I was trying to be like Heracles. It, it doesn't hurt much."

Dip was about to explain but Cerberus held up his hand. "I know of the Labours. He and I have been talking all evening."

Taking hold of Odysseus' arm, Cerberus gently popped it back into place.

"This will not happen to you again. Jackal, Wolf, lay down your weapons. I gave my orders and I expected them to be followed."

Wolf obeyed immediately but Jackal scowled and hesitated. "It is not what your father wants. He was very clear in the market."

Cerberus cut him off with a wave of his hand. "One day I will command my own army. My father had better get used to the idea. Now, drop your sword."

Jackal bowed slightly and dropped his sword, but Dip could still see his eyes. They remained fixed on Cerberus.

"Good. Wolf, bring the bag."

Wolf ran back to the middle of the stadium and hefted a large linen sack onto his back. He struggled beneath its weight and let it topple off him once he returned. Upon impact the sack opened, its contents spilling out at Dip's feet.

"Armour," said Dip. "I thought you said we weren't going to fight."

"We aren't," replied Cerberus. "My sister lost to the Athenian runner in the sprints because of Apollo. That is the loss I am going to avenge. We will race, you and I, as if the stadium were full of cheering spectators. However the victor will not feel the laurel on his brow. If you are victorious then you receive your friends and your freedom, at least for the moment. If I win then I get you and my father's command will be fulfilled."

Dip massaged his chest. It seemed that the Oracle's prophecy had arrived sooner than he expected and it was to be a sprint, not a long distance race. He nodded and began to remove his clothes.

Cassandra shyly turned her back as Cerberus and his hounds laughed.

"It may be the custom of the weaker cities to race without their tunics, but that is not how a Spartan runs. We run like we fight." He pointed to the armour scattered on the ground. "In full battle gear. Now get dressed and meet me at the starting line."

Dip bent and hefted the helmet. It was heavy and the bronze around the plume was dented. He set it aside and reached for foot coverings, also made of bronze. Then there was the shield. It was a defensive shield, large enough to cover most of his body. Dip looked to the sky.

"Apollo. You sheltered me all of these years and I have faith in your oracle, but I don't know how I can defeat Cerberus burdened by this armour. I'm not Heracles, I'll never be Heracles."

A hand brushed the tears from his cheek. "You won't have to, Dip. This is my fight, my race, and my fate. Yours is still ahead of you."

Cassandra lifted the helmet easily and put it over her head. Dip said nothing. He saw the hardness in her eyes.

"You're right, Cassandra. This is part of your destiny, not mine. Just make sure you win. Then we can all get out of here."

Cassandra stepped into the shinguards; they extended

from the ankles to just over the knees and were cut in the back to allow the knees to bend while running. Slipping her left arm through a band in the middle of the shield she gripped a rope tied to the inside edge and raised it to her shoulder.

"I believe the starting line is this way," she said.

CHAPTER TWELVE

A row of long and narrow stone slabs stretching across the field served as the starting line. Two continuous parallel grooves were cut into them, positioned as marks for the runner's feet, one slightly ahead of the other. Wooden poles separated the slabs into lanes and Cassandra and Cerberus lined up beside each other.

Cerberus turned to Cassandra. "Ready?"

She nodded back.

"Wait," said Dip. "I don't want any claims of trickery or misunderstanding used as an excuse for a Spartan defeat. Let's be clear on the rules."

"I do not need excuses. I am not my father. But if you insist, this is how the Spartan Armour race is run. First, we run two lengths of the track."

Dip sucked in his breath. One length was exactly two hundred paces. He had stepped it off many times when the stadium was empty.

Cerberus continued. "At the far end we turn at the kampter. Wolf will be stationed there to ensure the post has been touched, then it is a sprint back to the starting line where the winner is declared. Jackal will judge."

"No, not him. I don't trust him," Dip said.

"And I will not accept you," Jackal replied.

"I shall declare the winner," said a small voice. Odysseus looked to Cassandra and Cerberus. "I have their faith."

The two runners nodded.

"Then I shall act as starter," Jackal said. "One word of command only. You will recognise it when it is spoken. If someone starts before the command, the customary punishment shall also apply."

"And that is?" Dip said.

Jackal drew the edge of his sword across his throat. "Runners who attempt an unfair start against a Spartan only do it once. Anything else you need to know?"

Dip glanced at Cassandra, who shook her head and raised her shield. Both of her feet rested in the grooves, one foot slightly in front of the other. The knee of her front leg was bent and her weight was on her toes. Her rear foot and sole were completely flat. Her right arm stretched forward, palm pointed to the ground. Cerberus assumed the same position.

Jackal waved at Wolf positioned at the far end of the track, who swung his sword over his head in reply. Dip was about to say something to Cassandra, but when he saw the look in her eyes he thought better. It reminded him of Cerberus, eyes filled with hate for the enemy, darkness without light. It was the Cassandra Dip saw when she talked about her family and he was afraid.

A hand tugged at Dip's tunic. "Be ready Dip. Remember

your oracle. Athens must be warned. You must prove yourself still."

"What are you talking about Odysseus. How do you know about my oracle?"

The little boy's fingers dug into Dip's arm. "You know the way. Heracles survived his journey, so must you."

"Which journey, to where?" said Dip.

Odysseus did not reply, but stared at Jackal, who raised the sword high over his head. Both runners tensed, their eyes focused on the large wooden post at the end of the track.

"Hades," Jackal commanded, as he sliced the air with his sword. The race began.

Cerberus charged out of the start in the lead. Older and stronger, he was obviously used to carrying a shield while running. He held it steady while Cassandra's bobbed with each step. His smooth stride contrasted Cassandra's choppy steps and Dip could tell she was working hard, straining against the weight of the shield on her left arm. About halfway to the kampter, Cassandra's legs straightened and she raised the shield higher, and held it steady.

"That's it Cassandra," Dip yelled. "You can do it, catch him now."

Cerberus glanced over his shoulder and it was easy to see his frown as Cassandra gained ground. There were only a few paces between them as they neared the kampter when suddenly Cerberus darted into Cassandra's lane. Surprised, Cassandra stumbled trying to avoid a collision and lost her momentum. Cerberus sped on ahead, reaching the post several paces in front of his rival. With his free hand he grabbed the kampter and swung himself around. Wolf raised his sword to indicate the touch as Cerberus accelerated towards the finish.

"Not fair," Dip said. "He promised there wouldn't be any tricks."

"Nothing was unusual," said Jackal. "The girl should have realised they would have to merge lanes in order to touch the kampter. Cerberus just decided to change lanes earlier than expected. Spartans are known for their great battle tactics, she should have foreseen it. The victory is ours, no one can make up the distance between them. This time, I shall personally deliver you to Hades."

Dip leaned forward. They didn't know Cassandra.

Wolf's sword again waved, indicating Cassandra's touch. Cerberus' lead had stretched to ten strides, an almost insurmountable distance. Jackal bounced on his toes in front of Dip, baring his teeth.

Then, Cerberus's stride changed. His legs chopped at the ground and the massive shield tilted down, bouncing against his thigh. His mouth opened and closed, although no words were spoken.

He's getting tired, Dip thought. Just like the time he ran me down outside of the stadium. He was out of breath even though he caught me. He's fast, but not in top shape. Maybe those famed Spartan marches were at a walk instead of a run.

"Come on Cassandra. Remember the oracle."

Cassandra lifted her head. Even at a distance, Dip could see her features change, the darkness disappearing.

"No, no, it's not possible!" Jackal sagged and he lowered

his sword. "No one can move that fast."

Cassandra's free arm pumped up and down close to her body in rhythm with her legs and she ran upright, head held high. Then, the massive shield began to move. Not in frantic jerks like those of Cerberus, but in control, until both arms pumped at the same speed.

Dip bounced up and down. "Now she's running. Look at her go."

Cerberus was only forty paces from the finish and he knew he was in trouble. Throwing off his helmet he put on a new burst of speed. Cassandra responded with a shake of her head that sent her helmet flying and she too ran faster. Now she was smiling, almost laughing, as the gap between her and Cerberus closed.

At twenty strides to the finish she was on his heels. At ten she drew alongside and at that moment their eyes met. The blackness in Cerberus' eyes dulled and softened. A wide grin cut across his face and he charged forward. Cassandra matched him stride for stride and it seemed that they would cross the finish line together. But just before the finish, Cerberus' legs gave out on him, his arms windmilled and he dropped the shield, lost his balance and fell to the ground. Cassandra sped past, the victor. Dip jumped up and down in delight. "Did you see that, Jackal? Did you see that? That was amazing, that was incredible. What a race. I knew she could do it."

Jackal walked and stood over the puffing Cerberus, who extended his hand.

"A Spartan does not have to be helped to his feet," Jackal said, slapping it aside.

Wolf grabbed Dip from behind and pulled him towards Jackal. Odysseus ran to Cassandra, who was leaning against the stadium wall examining an object she had found in the cracks. Cradling it, she stepped out of her armour and ran to Cerberus with Odysseus following close behind. Reaching out, Cerberus took her hand and pulled himself to his feet. Interlocking his fingers with Cassandra's, he raised her hand to his cheek.

"It was a good race, fairly won. Back at the market, I knew you were favoured by Apollo, that is why I did not strike you. Now you have proven you can win without his help. You and your friends are free to go."

Dip shook himself free from Wolf, but Jackal shoved him aside. Stepping between Cassandra and Cerberus, he pushed Cerberus back to the ground and pressed the tip of his sword against his throat.

"What are you doing? Put your sword away, now!" Cerberus said. "Wolf, disarm him."

Wolf paused, then thrust his sword at Dip.

"You no longer direct us," Jackal said. "As I said before, your father does not want the boy to go free."

"You are my hounds. I picked you myself and I gave my word."

Cerberus was cut off by pressure from the tip of Jackal's sword.

"Our allegiance is to Sparta only. You should have disposed of the girl in the market, then you would not have humiliated yourself by losing this race."

"As I recall," Cerberus said. "You had a chance to finish her yourself, but failed."

Jackal scowled. "I will avenge that now." He raised his sword from Cerberus' throat and pointed it at Cassandra. "Wolf, give her your sword."

Wolf tossed his sword to Cassandra, who let it hit her arm and fall.

"I will not fight." She held out the object she had found. It was an egg-shaped stone, small enough to fit in her hand.

"This is Apollo's omphalos. Now that I have found it, I will not let it go."

"More nonsense," said Jackal. "The real one resides in the temple; there are no others, except of course for those sold by lowly merchants and," he nodded to Cerberus, "put in tripods holding babies unfit to be Spartans. To think I once admired you."

Jackal stepped on Cerberus' throat as the Spartan struggled to get up.

"Girl, fight me or you all die. What are you, a Helot?"

"Once," Cassandra said. "Not anymore. Look."

Over the horizon the sun began to push upward, its light reflecting brightly in Cassandra's eyes. "I will not fight."

"Then you are a fool."

Jackal swung and simultaneously, Dip leapt towards him. He grazed Jackal's arm causing the sharp edge of blade to rotate to its flat side, but its velocity unchanged, it slammed into the side of Cassandra's head and she crumpled, the omphalos still clutched in her hand.

Dip dropped to his knees beside Cassandra. Bending his head to her chest he listened for a heartbeat. There was none. His head started to pound and his eyes clouded over. Rage filled his heart as he sprang, but he was not quick enough. Jackal again swung his sword, and Dip fell to the ground and lay still.

CHAPTER THIRTEEN

Dip lifted his head. Cassandra lay motionless at his side and Odysseus sat cross-legged next to her. The moon's shadows were retreating as dawn replaced dusk.

"Where are they?"

The little boy pointed to a still shadowed section of seats. "Don't move. They are discussing our fate. In private, they believe."

Dip distinguished three bodies through the darkness. Two leaned back on the cut limestone slabs, while the other paced in front. Although high in the stadium, the acoustics carried the Spartan's argument easily to their ears.

"You should not have killed her Jackal. She was defenceless."

"I will fully report to your father. He can decide. Will you come willingly, or shall I have to subdue you like the others?"

"She can be saved you know."

Dip glanced up at the Spartans and back at Odysseus. The Spartan's angry tones had effectively masked the little boy's whisper.

"Think of Heracles, Dip. He travelled to Hades' realm, fought the guardian and returned safely. You can too. That is where Cassandra's soul now resides. Not permanently, not yet. She needs a hero. You can save her."

Dip looked into Odysseus' eyes as the sun's beams spilled over the side of the mountain and rolled over them both and up into the stands. Squinting against the rays, he saw Odysseus throw both arms up into the air. His withered arm straightened, forming the stylised V of the runner.

"Dip." Odysseus was staring directly into the sun, but he did not flinch. "Remember your oracle."

Dip closed his eyes and also raised his face to the rising sun. Bursts of light traced their path behind his eyelids and the priestess' eyes and her oracle filled his mind.

'Look to Odysseus to lead, run for your victory.'

Dip reached into the light and pulled Odysseus down, his arm shrinking and withering in his grasp.

"How do I get to Hades?"

Odysseus' massaged his damaged arm. "The Labours tell of many entrances and exits. It could be anything, a darkened doorway, a hole in the ground. All have one thing in common; Cerberus howling his challenge."

"I should have realised," Dip said. "Apollo showed me the way when I first came to Delphi."

He glanced at the sun's rays advancing on the Spartans. In a few moments they would be unable to see. Dip leaned over Cassandra, squeezed her hand, and pressed his lips to her ear. She did not smell of death.

"Have faith in me, Cassandra. I shall bring you back."

As the Spartans shielded their eyes against the sun, Dip stood up and placed his hands on Odysseus' shoulders.

"I know where an entrance is. Come run with me."

Sprinting to the edge of the stadium, they dashed up the steps and through the tunnel. To their right was the road leading back to the temple, in the opposite direction lay the top of the mountain. Dip knew his life at the temple was finished. He had to fulfil the oracle.

"This way," he said, and Odysseus followed him onto the winding road.

At every bend, Dip paused and listened. At the fourth, he heard them. Three, or maybe only two hounds barking. It didn't matter. Let them come, he thought. They are the least of my concerns.

Dip led Odysseus a little further down the road, arriving at the laurel trees. Selecting the two largest he plunged through, dragging Odysseus with him. Up the path they ran, coming to the mouth of the cave. Odysseus ran in, knelt by the stream and let the waters flow over his arm.

"Is this it?" Odysseus pointed to the cavern into which the stream flowed.

"Listen," Dip said.

Odysseus took two steps into the cavern. Above the sounds of swirling waters, faint yips and screams reached him.

"The real Cerberus?"

Dip nodded. "I've known about this place since I was a child, but I've never had the courage to enter."

"Or a reason," Odysseus said.

Now the barking grew louder, this time from the road.

Dip reached up and touched the runner etched above the tunnel's entrance. "We have Cerberus behind us and in front of us."

With one hand he ran his fingers over the mosaic tiles of Heracles still in the pocket of his tunic and with his other he grasped Odysseus' good arm and led him into the darkness.

CHAPTER FOURTEEN

The stream and tunnel soon widened and although they were far from the entrance, the light had not dimmed. Overhead, pinpoints of light flickered from the ceiling like sparks from a dying fire. With each step the ceiling receded until there was no difference between it and the night sky, the sparks intensifying into tiny flames as brilliant as any star.

Spray from the river coated their tunics as they balanced against the cave's wall. Wiping his eyes, Dip pulled Odysseus down beside him. Ahead, the waters smashed up against the bank, flowing over the narrow path before sucking back to the river.

Pointing down the path, Odysseus shivered, as if a cold breeze struck him in the face. "Terrors, besides Cerberus, guard the Underworld. The Labours tell of Heracles' descent, of his test. Perhaps if we both are silent they will not be disturbed."

Dip felt a rush of wind, doubled over in pain and doubt and clutched his heart. Through tears he turned on Odysseus and grabbed him by the shoulders.

"How can this be? You're only a child with a hero's name, The Labours is just a story, and Heracles is a myth; maybe once, a man like you and I, but he died a long time ago. He didn't join the gods. What are we even doing here? Cassandra is dead. Why don't we just go home?" Dip sank to his knees.

"There is no home for you," Odysseus said. "Or me. At least not yet. You've had the priestess all these years. What about me? My parents never cared. They found me when I was a baby, shaved my head to mark me as theirs and kept me to work the fields. When my arm proved too much of a burden they turned me out. The first night I slept in a field covered in straw. I woke in the middle of the night bathed in light. Stars streaked across the sky as if in a race. One star stumbled, then fell, landing almost at my feet. The breath of air it created knocked me over. I awoke warmed by Apollo, and the stories of the heroes and gods filled my mind. Since that time they've been the part of me that's kept me safe, led me to Delphi. I came to the temple and found you, Dip. All I know is that it is Apollo's will. Follow the path Dip, have faith. We can't go back."

Dip hung onto Odysseus' good arm, pulling himself to his feet. The boys hugged the wall and crept down the path. Water from the river ran over their toes. It was warm, almost hot against their skin. Dip, in the lead, peered through the spray and stopped.

The path divided into two. A crude wooden bridge crossed the river on their left, ending alongside a towering cliff and the waters beside it were still. On the right the path continued to be overrun with water, the cliff half as tall. A large overhang partially covered the face of a cave. In the distance another bridge connected the two paths again.

"This way," Dip said, pulling Odysseus onto the bridge. "It's drier, less chance of slipping."

"No! Not that way." Odysseus wrenched himself free and jumped onto the other path. "Move over here, quickly, quickly!"

Dip ran to Odysseus. "What is it? What's wrong?"

Odysseus pointed to the calm waters on the far side of the river. "Charybdis."

"And to the right. Is it?"

"Yes." Odysseus glanced upwards. "Scylla."

"Well," Dip said, "you know everything about the gods and their spawn. This is it Odysseus, this must be why Apollo chose you. Guide me. Save us. Which path did the hero, Odysseus choose?"

"No one knows that part of the story," Odysseus said, shrugging his shoulders.

"What! We have to choose between two monsters and you don't know. Did you make all of this up? Anybody can study the gods, hear the stories. Is that what you did? You're as useless as your arm."

Odysseus turned and ran along the watery path. Too fast.

"Slow down," Dip shouted. "I'm sorry, I didn't mean it."

Odysseus stopped and Dip caught up to him. "Listen, you're my friend and I'll believe whatever you say. Just don't run from me again."

"It wasn't you I was running from. Look."

Behind them, edging along the wall, was Cerberus and his hounds. They stopped at the split in the path. Wolf crossed the bridge and Jackal and Cerberus continued on.

"We had better go," Dip said.

"Carefully," added Odysseus, "and quietly."

Because of the bends in the trail and the spray it was difficult to see how far behind them Cerberus and Jackal were. However it worked in their favour too. The Spartans could not see either. Every few paces the waters rose, covering the path and Dip hugged the wall and held onto Odysseus to keep him from being swept into the river. It took all of his strength and concentration, so much so he did not notice the small dark figure across the stream.

Wolf's howl filled the air. The drier, wider path enabled him to catch up and he was within sight of the second bridge.

"Jackal, Cerberus, I see them, just ahead of you." His voice rose over the churning waters. "We've got them now."

Picking up a stone he threw it towards them, but it fell far short into the middle of the river.

Odysseus' eyes widened. "He shouldn't have done that. Now we'll really have to hurry."

Before they could move, Cerberus and Jackal sprang out of the mist behind them. Cerberus pinned Dip to the cliff, while Jackal knocked Odysseus down and put his sword to the boy's throat. Odysseus' head skimmed the surface of the water.

Dip struggled against Cerberus' grip but the Spartan was

much stronger and held him fast.

"Let him up. He's too close to the water."

Jackal shook his head and grinned. "It's about time he had a bath. Besides, with his arm, he could not be a warrior. Sparta has no use for that kind. Right, Cerberus?"

Jackal pushed Odysseus' head under the water, holding it until the boy's thrashing threatened to knock them both in. He jerked Odysseus back on the path, staring at his hair washed clean by the river. It was blood red, matching that of Hades and Cerberus.

"What's this, you even dare to have hair like our commander. Cerberus, this is the opportunity to redeem yourself. I will give you the privilege of removing this filthy affront to your father."

Cerberus released Dip and took a step towards Jackal, levelling his sword.

"Release him Jackal." There was no mistaking the menace in his voice, and Jackal relaxed his hold.

Odysseus tried to squirm free but the Spartan pulled him back down, this time putting his knee on Odysseus' weak arm.

"What's the matter with you Cerberus? You know what's expected of a Spartan. You took your baby brother into the hills and left him for the wolves. What was wrong with him anyway?"

Cerberus lowered his sword and fell back against the face of the cliff. He brushed tears from his eyes.

"I thought I was acting like a full Spartan warrior, a man, but no one saw me cry. My brother's left arm was withered."

Cerberus gathered himself and stretched one arm to Odysseus. "Forgive me Odysseus, I was wrong. My father was wrong. It was not Apollo's judgement and now that I have found you, I will not make that mistake again. As I said, Jackal, let my brother go."

"Stop it," Dip said. "Both of you. Look at the water, it's Charybdis."

Cerberus understood immediately. As Jackal turned to the water, Cerberus pounced on him, threw him off Odysseus and dragged both up against the cliff wall. Waving his arms wildly, he tried to signal Wolf to back off his path. Wolf just bounced up and down and waved back, still celebrating what he thought was the capture of Odysseus and Dip.

"The Pool," Cerberus said. "Watch out!"

Wolf couldn't hear. A small whirlpool had begun to grow in the middle of the river, accompanied by loud sucking noises. Within seconds the swirling waters expanded, whipping up pellets of stinging water that smashed against the cliff. Dip and Jackal crouched and covered their faces, while Cerberus threw his body over Odysseus, absorbing the brunt of the punishment.

The whirlpool began to move towards Wolf, its vortex expanding and contracting like the mouth of a ravenous beast. Wolf tried to run but the whirlpool was too fast. It intercepted him, overrunning the path. Stung by the spray, he dropped to his knees, then fell face first into the heart of the vortex. The sucking noise quickly abated and the whirlpool moved back to the centre of the river, contracted and disappeared.

Jackal was the first to recover. Moving away from the wall he stepped on Cerberus' wrist, pressing his arm and sword to the ground.

"I don't know what that was, but Wolf should not have run, and you were a fool to save me. A Spartan never gives up the advantage." He lifted his sword high.

Cerberus struggled to free his arm. "Don't you know? I was paying attention when we were taught the tales of Homer. Our gods walk among us, they are more powerful than any mortal."

Jackal lowered his sword. "I seem to remember something about Charybdis." He pulled at his ear. "Didn't Odysseus have to choose a path between two monsters? The whirlpool and something?"

Jackal paused. "The other I don't remember. No matter. I am a Spartan. We are the mightiest warriors in Greece. Nothing can defeat us. Not even the gods or their monsters. My teachers had nothing to offer me."

Sneering, he again raised his sword. "Prepare to die."

Odysseus glanced up at the cave above them and back at Jackal. His pupils in his eyes shone briefly with flecks of yellow. "Do not mock your teachers," he said. "You should have paid more attention to your studies."

Cerberus wrenched himself free and along with Dip and Odysseus, flattened against the face of the cliff as a loud grinding noise filled the air.

Jackal didn't have time to move. Six dogheads each on serpentine necks snapped around him. Three rows of teeth from each set of jaws ground relentlessly, ribbons of saliva hanging from their lips. Even though all were attached to the same body hidden overhead in the cave, they moved independently, each wanting Jackal for itself.

Jackal struck at one head, his sword piercing a lightless eye. Screaming in pain the head retreated to the cave, taking Jackal's protruding sword with it. The other heads now had Jackal completely cut off. For a moment they hung, suspended in front of him, then they attacked. Growling and snarling, one head clamped onto his right arm. Another took his left and two grabbed his legs. Jackal thrashed wildly, but as they lifted him off the path the last head rushed at him and bit hard into his torso. Jackal hung limp as he was hoisted into the cave's mouth.

"Hurry," said Odysseus. "He won't make much of a meal."

Linking arms, the three boys shuffled along the cliff until they reached the end of the second bridge. At this point the trail widened and moved away from the cliffs and they ran shoulder to shoulder until they stopped at a small grassy area bordering the river.

Cerberus took Odysseus' weak arm and cradled it. "Safe at last."

"Only on this side of the river." Odysseus pointed to the far bank.

The river had widened and it was difficult to see across, a fog shrouded the now calm waters.

"Hades' realm," Dip said.

Odysseus nodded. "Cassandra's soul rests with the others there; you alone can bring her back. You must fulfil your oracle, Dip. There are many exits as well as entrances to the Underworld. We will find our way home."

Cerberus stepped forward and grasped Dip's hand, then put his arm around Odysseus, tousling his hair. "Good luck. I will make sure my brother is safe. I abandoned him once. Never again."

Dip felt unusually calm. The black waters of the river beckoned him and he was not scared. As he moved towards the ash covered sands, a small boat emerged from the fog. Hewn in the shape of a snake, it was piloted by a single figure hooded in black robes. It slid onto the beach and Dip leaped into the bow.

Deep growls cut through the fog, rocking the boat, and as Dip hung onto the three-headed dog cut into the prow he nodded goodbye to his friends. The ferryman poled back into the river.

Cerberus awaits, Dip thought. Soon we will meet.

CHAPTER FIFTEEN

"I am Charon," the ferryman said. "You are privileged, few other mortals have been allowed passage to Hades."

Shoving his pole into the murky water, Charon strained against the waves. Bits of burning ash fell on Dip's hand, hardening quickly. Dip stuck his hand in the river, trying to scrape it off.

The ferryman threw back his hood and shook his head. His hairless, pale flesh moved about his face, the eyes, nose and mouth, sliding from one side to the other.

"Noooo," he said, the sound slurring through the fog.

Laying down the pole, he put both hands on his face, halting the moving flesh and pressed his features back into place.

"Hands out of the water please. Eels abound here. Not tame ones like in the world of the living. I too was once a desolate soul, being ferried across, not unlike you. Except I was dead. The ferryman was quite unpleasant and complained about his fate - insulted Hades. A gust of wind capsized us. Tossed us into the water. The eels ripped the ferryman apart. Hades barred his soul from the underworld; only then he had need of a new ferryman. Hades used the ferryman's leftover flesh to piece me together, but there were a few complications. As you saw, flesh does not fit as easily on shadow as bone. 'Touched by the gods,' Hades told me."

Charon cast his eyes about. "Mind you, I'm not complaining."

Dip quickly put his hands in his lap.

Gathering up his pole, Charon thrust it back into the water. "What about you, have you been 'touched' as well?"

Dip put his hand over his heart. "Perhaps. This is part of my oracle. Apollo's will. Like Heracles, I'm going to enter the Underworld. I've come to rescue my friend's soul."

The ferryman grunted at his pole. "You don't resemble Heracles in stature. Then again, looks aren't my best feature either. Strength is not always a measure of courage."

As they neared the shore, the fog turned into a grey haze and Dip could taste the grit on his tongue. Steering into a small cove the ferryman drew the boat alongside a narrow wooden dock charred in several spots.

"Sudden fires are not unknown here, stay on the path."

Three long, fearsome howls rolled over the boat, followed by a high pitched squeal of terror.

"You're in luck. Cerberus has already caught his supper. He'll probably be napping. To reach the souls of the dead you must follow the cracked path past his lair and travel a great distance to another river at the far edge of Hades' realm. The souls of the dead come there to drink. You will find your friend there. That is, if you make it beyond Cerberus."

Dip jumped onto the dock avoiding the weakened sections.

The ferryman poled away from the shore. "I shall not wish you luck. Whether you triumph or fail, I know we will meet again. I see every mortal soul after it dies."

Dip leapt from the dock to the land. Its surface was bare, black, hard packed earth. Ahead of him was a narrow path riddled with tiny fissures. Bouncing on his feet a couple of times he jogged to the path. "Don't count on seeing me again," he said quietly. "This is not my home."

Dip sat down and bending at the waist, grabbed his ankles. Feeling the tension on his hamstrings, he relaxed his stretch and stood, slowly extending the distance between his feet until the muscles in his upper thighs stretched and relaxed. He repeated these exercises several times until a familiar, comfortable, looseness and strength enveloped him.

I'm ready for you Cerberus, he thought. Now I know what my oracle meant. "Challenge Cerberus," the Oracle told me. "Run for your victory." This must be the run I've been training for since I came to the temple.

One final bend at the waist and Dip was off, jogging slowly. Low hills marked the horizon with the path curving between them. After a few minutes of comfortable running all of his muscles had loosened and he came upon a massive cavern. Deep, rhythmical breathing punctuated by muted yips reached him. Cerberus was asleep.

Dip stared into the mouth of the cave. Pains shot through his chest but he ignored them. Picking up a particularly sharp and ragged stone about the size of his fist, he threw it at the coiled form. Six pairs of eyes flipped open and three sets of jaws howled in pain.

Challenge accepted. Dip leaned into his runner's stance and began to run. It's time to fulfil the oracle. If my strategy works.

As he ran down the path he stole a glance at the real Cerberus emerging from the cave. The monstrous three-headed dog's jaws stretched wide, showing wicked rows of white teeth about the length of Dip's fingers. Each head had its own thick neck, encircled by a ribbon of smaller snakes which bit at its host, further enraging it.

Cerberus' body was covered with sparse black fur, which matched the blackness of the ground and sky, except in singed areas where patches of oily skin showed through.

Cerberus' six eyes locked onto Dip's, the monster shaking the ground with his challenge, then it chased him.

No. It's coming too fast. He increased his pace and checked over his shoulder. The distance between them was lessening.

Dip started to sprint, knowing he could only do so for a short distance. He was afraid to turn his head again, realising it would slow him down. Cerberus' panting echoed… coming closer… almost on top of him… foul breath…teeth brushing his heels… too fast … can't keep this speed up … no… can't help it… slowing, slowing now…where's Cerberus? … why hasn't he struck?

Puffing hard, Dip slowed to a jog and looked over his shoulder. Cerberus was about fifteen paces behind, all three heads drooping with their tongues hanging out. Even the snakes had wilted and were lying flat.

No stamina. Now I have him.

Dip continued to jog until he regained his breath. The gap between the two increased to about thirty paces and when Dip saw Cerberus gaining strength, he increased his pace accordingly until the three tongues again panted and the snakes stilled.

All I have to do is keep this up until he drops, or until I'm finished. Apollo's raven taught me how to race, how to pace myself. I will not fail.

The two ran steadily for thirty minutes, then an hour. At times Cerberus tried to take a shortcut outside of the path, however flames leapt up from crevices in the soil, singing him, forcing him back on the trail.

Ahead, between two hills lay the river, its surface calm and dark. As they neared, Dip could see shimmering faces floating to the surface.

Cerberus was tiring. At times he stumbled and his massive chest skimmed the ground, but he always pulled himself up and came forward. Dip's heart beat faster and he began a final sprint. Cerberus also coiled and leapt.

Using every last bit of strength, Dip pushed his legs ahead and dodged to the side. Cerberus, with one final scream, flew by him and landed half in and half out of the river, then lay still. Too exhausted to lift themselves, Cerberus' three heads whimpered and snakes included, lapped at the water.

An excited hum rose from the river. The faces swirled, came together and moved across the surface in a whirlpool of eyes. It rushed towards him. As it neared, its revolutions slowed and it dissolved into separate forms, people yes, but transparent beings, all with shocked looks on their faces.

The souls jostled one another trying to get a glimpse of the defeated Cerberus and they tried in vain to grasp Dip's hand. Crying out in despair they passed around and through him. Dip peered through them, desperately searching in the throng for one face alone.

"We must go now," said one of the souls. "It pains us to be this close to the living."

His lined face bore the scars of many battles. "I have defeated many, but not one such as this. You have proven, like Heracles, you do not belong here. It would have been my honour to have fought beside you. Farewell."

Souls began to move, their faces breaking apart.

"Not yet," Dip said. "Cassandra, Cassandra. Where are you?"

Out of the swirling bodies, Dip felt the solid grasp of flesh against his hand. Cassandra's face hung motionless in front of him and she struggled against the pull of the now shapeless souls.

Cassandra pushed her other hand through the vortex. Clenched in her palm was the omphalos.

Dip closed both of his hands over hers. He tried to pull her free, but the forces against him were too great. Her face expanded and her hands began to lose their substance. As Cassandra's fingers faded, his own touched the omphalos and the priestess' voice echoed in his mind.

"Remember your oracle and Apollo. Proclaim your victory, Dip. Shout it and your spirit will rise."

Dip shut his eyes and yelled, "Nike!" Light pierced his closed lids and he felt the ground shake. The heaving soil tossed him into the river and he flailed, struggling for the shore. A giant eel snapped at his toes and he kicked hard, then his hands closed on a ribbon of snakes and he emerged from the water clinging to Cerberus' oily back.

Calmly, the monster waited until the tremors subsided, then picked its way back along the path, skirting blocks of obsidian thrusting through the ground and newly formed crevices, until it reached the mouth of its cave.

The three heads screamed out their challenge and Dip covered his ears. Hearing no reply, it entered the cave and coiled, the heads and snakes lying themselves down and closing their eyes as one. Dip slid off.

A dot of light appeared in a tunnel at the far end of the cave and he ran towards it. After a few minutes the tunnel narrowed and rose, forcing him first to walk, then climb as it turned into a shaft. Struggling for handholds he ascended to the light. Just as he reached a hand to the top, the ground shook again. Pulling himself through he found himself high on the side of the mountain. Far below he saw the stadium shaking and several Spartan warriors swaying outside.

Then as the quake stopped, he heard the thunder and cried out as boulders raced past him, down the mountain.

Dip sprinted down the slope onto the road, turning to see more rocks overrun the shaft and plunge after him. On he ran until he felt the shaking slow and subside. Glancing around, he fell to his knees and cried. His laurel trees were crushed, his cave and stream completely blocked.

Wiping the grime from his face, he continued down the mountain to the stadium and seeing no Spartans around, plunged through the tunnel. Exhausted, he stumbled at the top of the steps, tumbling down to the playing field.

Blood flowed from the side of his head. A monstrous shadow blocked the sun and Dip tried to roll away from it. As the shadow moved and took shape, bright sunlight flowed over him.

"There is no need to be afraid young one, the Spartans have gone," boomed Titan.

Gentle hands held him and a warm cloth was pressed up against his wound.

"Thank you Dip," Cassandra whispered into his ear. "You brought me back."

CHAPTER SIXTEEN

Titan carried Dip outside the stadium and set him down on a stone bench in the outer courtyard. Cassandra sat beside him. She removed his dressing, now caked with dried blood and replaced it with a clean piece of tunic.

Dip began to speak, but Cassandra put her hand over his mouth. "Save your strength, Dip. I've told Titan and Stratus about Odysseus and your odyssey, how you challenged the real Cerberus, and your escape from the underworld."

"How do you know, how could you know? You were just a soul. It seems unreal, but I know it wasn't. I've changed, Cassandra. I may not be Heracles, but I'm no longer a temple rat."

Dip stood and slowly raised himself into a warrior's stance. Ripping the bandage from his head, he faced Stratus and Titan. "Believe or do not believe. It doesn't matter to me. I crossed the river Styx. I defeated Cerberus. And I saved Cassandra."

Stratus looked back and forth at the two youths. "I have no doubts about your adventure Dip, or about Cassandra. I've travelled all over Greece and beyond, fought unimaginable creatures."

"Ahem," Titan interrupted, rolling his eyes. "Been rescued from unimaginable creatures."

"Yes, yes, if you must," Stratus said. "Rescued and all that. As I was saying, beings and places exist beyond anyone's imagination. Whether spawned by the gods or one's mind, they exist, because people believe. Titan and I do not question other's realities, we accept and experience them. Then we move on."

"Usually after sampling the grapes indigenous to the land," Titan said. "We would have come sooner, but this fool of a poet was late. Out finding more wine."

"Nonsense, I was gathering more information about the race. As it happened, Miltiades was quite well-guarded, evidently worried about retribution from Hades. It took quite a while even to talk to his aides."

"Of course you had to have a few sips of wine while you waited."

Stratus stifled a burp. "What matters is that Titan and I arrived in time to rescue Cassandra."

"You, Stratus?" Dip said.

Cassandra tossed her head and laughed. "Titan did the rescuing. The earthquake shook me awake and I saw that all of you had gone. Before I could get up, four Spartans sprinted into the stadium and surrounded me. The tremors stopped and Titan appeared, leaping the length of the steps to the field."

Stratus broke in. "Yes, and when they saw me, all four scattered and fled."

"Not quite," said Cassandra. "Titan swept two off their feet with his legs and kicked them across the field. Then he grabbed the other two, flipped their helmets off, knocked their heads together and flung them on top of their comrades. And off they ran."

"Yes," said Stratus, "and as they passed I struck each on the backside with the flat end of my sword."

"That would have been difficult Master poet, considering you were still hiding behind a seat."

"I dropped my sword. Could have happened to anybody."

"Enough, enough," Dip said. He touched his head. The flow of blood had stopped and the ache was diminishing. "I'm grateful you showed up although I'm not sure how you knew."

"That was my doing," Cassandra said. "When I left you at the banquet, I thought we might need some sort of back up. Not that I didn't have confidence in my own abilities, but I have never trusted any Spartan. I found Titan and the rest…"

"I will compose an ode." Stratus straightened. "No, a heroic poem about a young woman and a boy who has become a young Heracles, victorious against overwhelming odds, of course with the help of a courageous poet."

Titan rolled his eyes. "Shall I escort you somewhere safe? You can stay with us if you wish."

"No," Dip said. "I still have part of my oracle left. The Athenians must be warned about Sparta. If they rely on Sparta for help during the Persian invasion all shall be lost. I must win that race."

"Oh yes, Apollo's Race." Stratus knocked himself on the head. "It is to be run today. In a couple of hours actually. This will be your only opportunity to give your message from the Oracle to Miltiades. He is heavily guarded, no one can approach him, except for the winner of the race. Miltiades will reward him personally. The Athenian delegation is leaving immediately afterwards."

Titan stroked the side of Dip's head with one massive finger. "Are you sure you are up to it? I could overpower any guards, and force Miltiades to listen to you."

"No. This is the last part of my oracle. I alone must warn the Athenians about Sparta's plan. It is my destiny and I am responsible for it."

"I'll ask one last favour," Cassandra said. "But first, there is something I must get."

She dashed back into the stadium, then re-emerged moments later carrying the bag of armour she had worn during the race. She tossed it at Stratus, whose knees buckled under its weight. Titan picked it up with a finger and slung it over his shoulder.

Holding out her hand, she displayed the stone egg she had found.

"My omphalos belongs in Apollo's temple and there is one more Spartan I must deal with, but I need your help Titan. What do you say?"

"Of course we'll help," Stratus broke in. "Anything for our friends."

Titan snorted. "He has heard of the famed temple wine cellar, the libations donated over the centuries by ardent disciples."

Stratus kicked at the dirt. "You must admit, the thin air up here does dry out one's throat."

He started off down the road. "Come on, don't be tardy. Now's not the time to shy from battle."

CHAPTER SEVENTEEN

As the companions rounded a bend, they saw several Athenian soldiers sitting on a large wooden post lying in the middle of the road. Sweating and passing around a dripping waterskin, they waived amiably.

"The kampter?" Dip said.

One soldier nodded. "Miltiades wants it set close to the top of the mountain to mark the turn around. The rest of us have to make sure there's no interference with the runners." He wiped his brow. "This altitude is too much for me."

"You're just fat and lazy," one of the others called out. "You should be slim, like that one." He pointed to Dip. "How about it boy, are you entering the race?"

Dip nodded.

"Maybe by the time we dig this thing into the ground, we'll all be fit enough to run like you. Time to go lads." He laughed at the groans as the Athenians struggled to lift the pole to their backs. "Don't worry lads, Miltiades himself told me we were leaving for home right after the race. Now come on, we have to have this up within the hour."

With a wave of hands the soldiers trudged up the road.

Within the hour! Dip thought. He jogged briskly down the road, the others close behind. After a couple of minutes, they came on the temple. It seemed empty, deserted.

"They must all be gathering in the marketplace for the start," Cassandra whispered.

"Not all," Dip said.

One of red-robed priests emerged at the top of the temple steps. Spotting them, he turned and rushed back inside.

The four companions ran up the temple steps and with Cassandra in the lead, burst through the antechamber doors and into the Oracle's room. Kheerna stood next to the tripod, the three priests kneeling beside her, bending over a mixture of laurel leaves, wood chips, and slender limbs piled in a pit.

Kheerna barely glanced at them. "You're too early. These fool priests tell me the boughs must be lit, must produce the white smoke before I can be declared the Oracle. Idiots. The wood is green, it will never light."

She kicked at one priest desperately scraping flint on flint, producing a few, scant sparks. "Come back later. I'll answer your questions then."

"We're not here for our oracle." Cassandra drew a sword from the bag. "Step away from the tripod."

Kheerna looked up. A look of sheer delight crossed her face. "A sword. You have a Spartan sword."

Cassandra dumped the sword and the rest of the armour onto the floor, and Kheerna jumped down from the chamber, embracing and caressing each piece with affection.

Running her finger along the edge of the sword's blade she looked up at Cassandra.

"I'll fight you for it."

Cassandra swept her arms around the room. "And give up this?"

Kheerna spat in the direction of the priests and pulled at her gown. "This fancy garment does not scratch and pull at me like a warrior's tunic should. I would much rather be weighed down by armour than questions. I said I would fight you for it. I'll fight all of you for it," and she raised herself up, gathering the folds of her gown in one hand.

"What about Hades," Cassandra said. "His plans. The white smoke."

"My father's a fool. I should be commanding his army. Ruling Sparta is my destiny, why should I be stuck in this marble tomb?"

Cassandra walked up the steps and sat on the tripod. The priests rose and reached to remove her, but Titan's growl resonated off the walls and they threw themselves back on the ground.

"There is no need to fight." Cassandra gripped the edges of the tripod and looked straight at the Spartan. "Take the armour. Leave and chase your destiny."

"Gladly," Kheerna said, as she gathered the armour into the sack. "My father shall suffer for this." She pointed to the priests. "You three come with me, I'll need attendants."

Evidently, the priests had had enough as well. Screaming and throwing their arms into the air, they rushed past Kheerna, who kicked at them as she hefted the armour onto her back and strode from the room.

Cassandra motioned to Dip, who walked to her side. She held out her hand and he gripped it, intertwining his fingers with hers.

"When I sat on the tripod before, holding the bits of shattered stone, I had a glimpse of my fate in the underworld. You were part of it Dip. I knew you would save me. Now that I found my own, whole omphalos, my future is clear. Apollo drew me here Dip, to become his oracle. Cerberus has found his brother, but mine is still lost to the Spartans. This sanctuary is now my home and I will find a way to bring Castor here."

Raising the egg shaped stone high over her head, she brought it down quickly, striking a glancing blow against the edge of the tripod. Sparks showered onto the auric leaves, igniting them in a burst of white flame and white smoke immediately curled up through a shaft cut into the temple roof.

"Titan and Stratus will protect me, establish me as priestess before they move on. This is the last you'll see of me Dip. You do not belong here. Your oracle still must be fulfilled."

"Apollo's Race," Dip said.

Cassandra smiled and looked up at the white smoke rising into the clouds. "Go. Be like Heracles. Prove yourself to the Athenians. Race Apollo for your victory."

CHAPTER EIGHTEEN

At least thirty boys jammed into the far end of the market, pushing and shoving, jockeying for a position close to the starting line scratched in the dirt. Dip recognised a few of them, sons of local merchants or farmers. They did not befriend him when he came to Delphi and they ignored him now. The others were sons of diplomats or dignitaries in for the Games.

Most of the carts and stands had been removed, allowing room for the spectators to view. The race had been inserted as the final event of the games and attracted a large crowd, all of whom would rush to fill the stadium after the start.

"Pretty exciting isn't it?" A tall, slim boy about Dip's age hopped beside him. "I couldn't believe it when my father told me about the race. A chance for a laurel wreath! Someday I'll be in the Games representing my city. Did I tell you I was from Corinth."

Dip moved away and the boy turned to another nearby competitor and struck up a conversation. The last thing Dip wanted to think about was where he was from. He didn't have a home. He didn't belong anywhere.

No more, he told himself. Time to focus on the race. I must fulfil the oracle, warn Athens of Sparta's plan. That's all that is important now.

As he bent over for a final stretch, the throng of boys and crowd parted. Miltiades, escorted by several soldiers, walked to the starting line. He raised his hand in the air and everyone hushed, but only for a moment. Another rumble rolled through the market as Hades and his bodyguard pushed forward. In front of them was Cerberus, a purple welt swollen under his eye.

One hand covering his bruise, Cerberus ran to Dip's side.

"Why are you here?" Dip said. "Is your father forcing you to capture me? Has he captured Odysseus? He must realise it would cause too much of a disturbance and the Athenians would become involved. Your father can't risk that."

"I know, that isn't it. Odysseus is with Titan and Stratus at the temple. My father has ordered me to run. He said I have shamed him enough and only by winning this race will I prove I am a true Spartan. If I don't I am not to come back. He said he would deal with you personally after the Athenians leave."

Cerberus stretched his arms behind his back. "Now be quiet, listen to the starter."

Miltiades raised his sword towards the sky. Everything stilled.

"A course has been marked out through the town and around and up the mountain. My men are positioned along the route to ensure no shortcuts are taken and," Miltiades stared at Hades, "no claims of trickery."

Dip relaxed a little. He would be safe from the Spartans, at least while the race was being run.

"The winner must complete the course before Apollo's chariot completes his journey across the sky and sun sets on the finish line in the stadium, where I personally shall crown the champion. Good luck to you all, may the gods run at your side."

"At the start stick with me," Dip whispered to Cerberus.

Miltiades dropped his sword and the pack of runners sprinted through the marketplace and down the road. Except for two. Dip and Cerberus ran slowly side by side, letting the lead group surge ahead. Hades stared at his son, shook his head in disgust and moved off.

"This is a long run," Dip said. "I know the route well. The strategy in a run like this is to conserve your strength, balance it out over the duration of the course, then use your reserves at the end."

"I understand." Cerberus matched Dip's smooth, steady pace. "Battle tactics are my speciality after all. The others are wasting their energies by sprinting at the beginning. They'll have nothing left at the end. How did you learn that?"

Dip thought back to the raven leading him, training him. "Just something I picked up when I was a child. Look, there's the pack, time to increase our pace."

At the outskirts of Delphi they passed the first few competitors, ten minutes later, another group of runners, some walking. As they made their way up the mountain all had been passed save for one, just ahead of them nearing the turn that would lead them down again and back to the stadium.

"I know that boy," said Cerberus. "He is an Arkadian, renowned for their endurance."

He was slightly built, with long legs. "You can defeat him Cerberus," Dip said. "He doesn't have your tenacity."

Cerberus was beginning to pant and fall behind. "Perhaps, but I can't keep up your pace Dip." He held out his hand and Dip gripped it tightly, then let it go. "I always knew you were going to win but I had to try. I won't be returning to Sparta with my father."

"Didn't he want you to become a general one day?"

Cerberus took a deep breath. "In the market, when I was about to strike Cassandra, she touched me and something happened. I was able to feel and see things within myself I had denied for the longest time. I knew then my destiny would not lie with my father. Hades has his daughter, and I, I have a brother now."

Cerberus stumbled and Dip reached to steady him. "Time for you to leave Dip. Time for you to increase your pace." He winked broadly. "Battle tactics you know."

Dip sped up the road, passing the Arkadian runner by a few paces, before reaching the post signifying the halfway point on the course. An Athenian soldier raised his sword indicating the touch and Dip ran down the road leading back to the stadium, the Arkadian close behind. Without turning his head, Dip sprinted. After a few minutes the footsteps behind him faltered, then faded, the Arkadian unable to meet Dip's challenge.

He allowed himself a self-satisfied smile. I hope that will exhaust him enough for you, Cerberus. Catch him now.

It had been almost two hours into the race and Dip continued to run strongly.

Not far to go. Just the temple to pass.

A few people lined the road, shouting encouragement. As the temple came into view he thought he saw Cassandra, but rays from the setting sun flashed off its walls, blinding him from everything except the road in front of him.

Wiping the tears from his eyes he prepared himself for the final sprint. Shadows covered the entrance to the stadium and he could see Apollo in his chariot sinking below the horizon. People unable to get into the stadium waved him forward. The tunnel leading to the playing field was brightly lit with torches and Dip, hearing the rumbling crowd, sprinted inside.

As he came through, the crowd stood and cheered, but he could feel the shadows snapping at his heels. Leaping down the steps three at a time he reached the playing field and sprinted around the track.

Coming to the kampter he touched it, turned and raced the last of Apollo's rays. Roars shook the ground as he crossed the finish line bathed in the full light of the sun. He had won.

An Athenian soldier escorted him halfway up the seats to the section reserved for dignitaries. Miltiades rose and took his hand.

"Congratulations. You have raced Apollo and won. I'm

sure Apollo himself must have blessed you with your speed. My sentries tell me except for two, all the others have dropped out. It takes courage and stamina to run that far that fast. If only my soldiers were as well-conditioned. Now tell me your name and the city you represent."

Before Dip could answer, more shouts broke out from the spectators. Cerberus and the Arkadian passed through the tunnel into the stadium, now fully lit by torches. Reaching the kampter together, they turned and began their final sprint side by side. Ten paces from the finish, the Arkadian's legs gave out on him and he sprawled face down on the track. Cerberus crossed the finish and with a wide grin on his face, sat down and waved up at Dip.

Dip turned back to the Athenian general. "I have something important to tell you about the Spartans. The Oracle sent me."

Miltiades scratched his beard. "A boy as a messenger from a dead Oracle? Perhaps. But first things first. I have a victor to crown. As I said, what is your name and what city do you represent?"

Dip hung his head. "My name is Dip, and I have no city to belong to."

"Raise yourself Dip. Surely that is a nickname, fit only for a boy. You have shown a man's, no, a hero's courage in winning this race. Use your real name and I will embrace you as my own."

Dip looked up at the Athenian General. "My name is Phidippides, sir."

Miltiades nodded to his vice-commander, Themistocles,

who placed the laurel wreath on Phidippides' head.

"Phidippides", Miltiades said, "you can call Athens your home now."

EPILOGUE

Phidippides' legs ached as he ran and he touched the wound on his side. Fortunately it was not serious, the Persian's spear had deflected off his shield.

No matter, he thought. It had been a total, glorious victory for Athens over the Persian army. Miltiades led the Athenian army brilliantly, using battle tactics never seen before. His troops were outnumbered two to one, but he surprised them by having a small group of soldiers sprint directly at the heart of the Persian army assembled shield to shield in a classic hoplite battle line across the plain.

Miltiades then sent the bulk of his force around the ends of the line and attacked from the rear. Caught off guard the Persian generals could not reassemble their troops and they scattered, only to be finished off by the pursuing Athenians.

A raven broke through the clouds above the mountain pass. It circled high above Phidippides then slowly descended, drawing even with Phidippides' head, matching his stride with the rhythmical flapping of its wings.

Phidippides did not break stride or veer from his path, but turned his head and spoke. "It all came to pass, just as the Oracle predicted, didn't it Apollo?"

"Almost all of it, Dip." The raven did not speak, its words filled Phidippides' mind.

"I tried, Apollo. On the eve of the battle Athens still had not received a reply from Sparta. The generals sent me. I ran a full day without stopping to again ask Sparta for help. They refused, claimed there was a religious festival going on and could not leave. Without resting I ran back and told the generals. Only Miltiades was not upset."

"You had given him the oracle," said Apollo. "He had faith."

Phidippides thought back to his friends. "It was you, wasn't it, Apollo? You were Odysseus."

"Yes. At times I did accompany Odysseus. The gods were aware of his strength at birth. It took us three days to persuade the Fates not to sever his thread."

The raven flew a little faster, causing Phidippides to speed up.

"Is he safe? I didn't have time to find him."

"Odysseus is with Cerberus, but they have yet to fulfil their oracle.

"From Cassandra?"

Phidippides could feel the heat from the sun intensify.

"Yes. She still resides in my temple, for now. Her prophecies pull at her."

"And me? What is to become of me?" Dip said. "Miltiades

took me in and treated me like his son, but Athens is not my home. I've even tried to be like Heracles, but I'm not him." Dip put his hand on his chest. "My heart is hurting me Apollo. It has as far back as I can remember."

"I know Dip. That is why I had your mother bring you to Delphi. So I could look after you. But I had to train you for your oracle, your test."

"Why did you involve Athens? Save them?"

"Your mother was Athenian. She prayed and sacrificed often to me. Unfortunately, I could not resist her. Gods and mortals were not meant to mix, Dip. The product is flawed. Only a few can be saved, and they must prove worthy."

Phidippides felt a sudden rush of warm air and before the raven drifted up towards the clouds, he managed to reach out and touch its back.

"Have I proven myself, Apollo?"

Apollo's voice echoed faintly. "Remember your oracle, Dip and your spirit shall rise, like it did from Hades. Race me one last time."

Phidippides ran through the pass, smelling the salt air of the ocean, seeing Athens spread out before him. The sun was setting and he had to reach Athens before it disappeared. He quickened his pace, ignoring the increasing pains in his chest. Word must have spread of his approach because he could see the gates of the city open and some of the council members waiting for news of the battle. He began his final sprint. The pounding and pain in his chest overwhelmed him just as he reached the first council member.

Victory or defeat, that's all they want to know.

"Nike," Phidippides shouted, thrusting his arms into the air as the last of the sun's rays crossed his chest. "We are victorious." Then he fell to the ground and lay still.

Dip jogged slowly up the side of the mountain. All the pain had vanished. Passing through a bank of clouds he could see two figures ahead of him, sitting on the grass, laughing and drinking. One was wearing a lionskin. The other rose and waved him forward.

"Father?" Dip said.

"Yes," said Apollo. "Come join us. You're home now."

AUTHOR'S NOTE

In 490 B.C.E., Persia invaded Greece. Athens, along with a few soldiers from the city of Platea, prepared to meet the Persian army camped on the plains of Marathon. The Athenians sent their greatest runner, Phidippides, to Sparta to get help. It took him a full day of running to reach Sparta, but when he arrived the Spartans refused to come out from behind their walls, claiming a religious festival could not be interrupted. Phidippides then ran back to Athens in one day.

Without Sparta the Athenian forces were heavily outnumbered and if they lost, then all of Greece may have fallen to the Persians. But one Athenian General named Miltiades employed a strategy never used before. He sent a small group of well-conditioned soldiers sprinting towards the centre of the Persian line. The rest of the Athenian forces swept around the ends of the Persian army, taking it by surprise and routing them. The Greek historian Herodotus reports that the Athenians had 192 dead compared to 6000 Persians. A marble treasury decorated with (among others) a sculpture of Heracles was later built by the Athenians at

Apollo's Temple in Delphi, commemorating their victory.

Legend has it the Athenians sent Phidippides sprinting back to Athens (at approximately the same distance as the modern marathon) to report the victory and when he arrived at the gates of the city he shouted 'Nike, we are victorious', then died. Today, many runners completing their first marathon shout 'Nike' as they cross the finish line in commemoration of Phidippides.

Although *Racing Apollo* is a work of fiction, it is based on these events.

CPSIA information can be obtained
at www.ICGtesting.com
Printed in the USA
LVOW01s0537180117
521259LV00026B/349/P